This Book is Dedicated

Thank you, for opening new worlds to me.

For my Wife,

Thank you for all that you are, and all that you do.

This wouldn't have been possible without you.

Thanks, Love.

All mention of persons and places is coincidental and unintentional. I thought I made them up.

The Blue Blood Mage

By Ben Pollard

Chapter One

I looked down over the edge of the cliff, my thoughts swirling like the dust devil off to my left. If I wasn't good enough, or ambitious enough; why did she want everything I'd worked for? I nudged a rockover the lip, watching it bounce off the cliff-face with a clatter. I took a deep breath, shook my head, then stepped back. Using someone else to measure my self-worth removed myself from the equation. Like working out: if it didn't take work, it would just be called out.

I took another few steps back. I chuckled. Falling to my death, accidentally, after I decided to live. Oh, the irony.

"I thought you were going to do it there for a minute Daniel," a voice said. A voice I knew well.

"I guess screwing my wife wasn't enough Jack?" I asked as I turned to face him fully. Handsome in a way I'd never match, he flipped his blond hair off his forehead. The comparison between us didn't bother me now, not in the way it did before.

He smirked. "Nah, Amanda is sure you still have something squirreled away somewhere." A sneer pulled the perfect symmetry of his face askew. "And I'm here to enjoy getting it from you."

"Damn Jack," I cocked my head to the side. "You sound like you want to fuck. I know I loosened her up a bit for you, but it can't be that bad," I said, shaking my head.

"You always thought you were smarter than everyone else," Jack growled out. "All that kung-fu shit don't make you a tough guy." His hands balled at his sides.

I nodded along. "It's Krav maga, but you're right, it doesn't." I put my hands behind my back and faced him fully. "It's a difficult thing deciding how to kill one's self." He opened his mouth, but I interrupted him. "How to do it, what is the most painful, what's the quickest?" I shook my head, tisking. "Jumping wasn't my first choice," I said as I pulled the Glock nine millimeter from my waistband and pointed at him. "That was my backup."

His mouth dropped open and he put his hands up.

"A surprising number of people survive headshots. Not many, but I didn't want to be one of them." I let all the crushing hopelessness I'd overcome fill my eyes and said, "You can walk away now, Jack. Enjoy all her money. Live. Or you can die, right here, right now."

His gaze met mine and whatever he saw there made the blood drain from his face. He took two stumbling steps back and he tripped, falling on his ass. He scrambled to his feet and dashed away around a bend and then lost to sight. Moments later a vehicle roared to life and a cloud of dust all that remained of my final relationships.

I pushed down my feelings to deal with the problems I had now. My planning didn't take into account that I might change my mind. If the gun and the fall didn't do the job, hiking out of the desert would be impossible. Water, shelter, food and only four hours of daylight left. Water first.

Water wasn't that far away, only a mile down into the canyon. There were pathways down to the river, I just needed to find one.

Three hours later I scooped river water with my hands and scrubbed the dust and dirt from my face. I scooted back and, using a driftwood stick, dug a hole half a meter from the riverbank. I dug three more similar holes spaced three meters apart going down river. The first hole filled with water by the time I finished with the last hole. The sediments would filter out things like Giardia and other parasites. The water was gritty, but it would do for now, until the solids settled to the bottom. I drank my fill then looked for something to use as shelter.

Bushcraft was a passion of mine. At least until I'd met Amanda. She said it took too much time away from our relationship and that I needed to put "us" first. Eventually I stopped going out into the wilderness. Even though I no longer practiced the craft, the knowledge stayed with me.

As I ranged upriver, I filled my left pocket with chert rock, keeping the biggest piece in hand. A little over a hundred meters from my waterholes I found a nice cave-like cut into the cliff's face. About ten meters deep and three high it would shelter me from the elements. I emptied my pockets at the entrance and continued exploring while I still had daylight.

I collected several handfuls of black Currant berries. Tart, but edible, they'd tide me over till morning. I hoped. I also gathered up some Coyote Willow branches for bedding, to keep me up off the ground. Some deadwood for a fire and I was set for the night.

I made a twig bundle and with the fist sized flint and a river rock (and bruised knuckles) had a fire going just before full dark. I laid back, twigs and branches poking me and got as comfortable as I could. Hands folded behind my head I watched the firelight play across the cave wall. Iridescent shapes glittered and almost made sense. A story played there, just out of reach, that I didn't find before sleep claimed me.

There is a different smell to the separate places of the world. The desert is dry, dusty. If thirst had a smell that's where you'd find it. So call me crazy, but even before I opened my eyes, I knew by the change in scents that I wasn't where I should be. It was wet, earthy and dank, in the way forests around the world smell after a summer rain.

I opened my eyes to darkness. With a small patch of, not quite as dark, past where my fire belonged. I reached for my gun then realized I didn't have clothes anymore. Why was I naked? Cold rock bit into my back as I shifted, my makeshift bed gone as well. I quietly got to my feet. My outstretched hands couldn't touch the sides of the cave. A halting step and my foot found something. It wasn't an animal, vegetable, or mineral. I probed at it with what Amanda called my "Monkey toes." Quick pain flashed through me until I built up enough anger to drive it away.

It felt like a book about the size of my hand. Keeping my eyes open as wide as they would go, I focused on the faint sense of the lightening of the dark up ahead, I squatted and retrieved it. Yup, a book. Leather bound. I was wrong, it was from an animal. I continued on trying to find the light at the end of this tunnel.

My hand touched the wall a split second before my face did, and a bright flash of pain made spots flash against the dark. I turned my head away and blinked rapidly. I could see a shadow of my hands waving against the darkness around in front of me now. My pace increased with my confidence. The path twisted and turned, but the strength of the light grew, until it blinded me. But, when my sight returned, I almost wished it hadn't.

A group of people had made a camp here. They'd been dead for a long time but… I leaned to the side and vomited. By the positioning of the skeletal remains I counted three females, one male, and two children. All had had their heads removed. The male, staked about a meter up, on the side of a wagon. The females were pinned down with stakes. Cleary, by the spread eagle positions, they'd been raped and murdered, the man forced to watch. I didn't want to think of the children. I vomited a little bile, all that remained in my stomach.

Chill rain on my back brought me out of my stupor and reminded me of my own precarious situation. I circled the remains of the family not wanting to disturb the grisly site. The side of the wagon was scorched, but not charred. More bodies lay tangled in death, but these wore rusted armor, and yellow skulls grinned out from under pot helms.

The door, propped shut with a rotting spear, kept it closed all this time. A hundred, maybe two hundred years? I'm not an expert. The increasingly frigid rain drove me onward. I knocked the dry rotted pole out of the way. I yanked the door open and a tingling sensation passed through me as I crossed the threshold. Not passed along my skin. Not raised goosebumps. Passed through me. My heart shuddered and my already queasy stomach threatened to rebel again. But, the feeling passed quickly.

The wagon must have been the family's living space. Three tiered bunks lined the walls to my left and right. They looked ready to sleep in. No dust or debris as one would expect from the amount of time suggested by the remains outside. A sitting area or family room occupied the far end with a pot bellied stove vented through the ceiling. Bright carpets and rugs gave the small space a touch of warmth and cheer even in the cold air.

Two trunks each sat along both sidewalls, with fire wood stacked along the far wall. I whispered my condolences to the family then opened the trunks. The first two held dresses, the third a drawstring tan breeches with white long sleeved open neck shirts. A black leather vest hung on a peg above the trunk. I took a breath then got dressed. The pants were a little short, but the waist fit after I tied the strings. The shirt had ties as well, but it fit tight already in the shoulders and chest. I looked like I came out of a Ren Faire reenactment. If not for the macabre scene outside I would have laughed.

The rain now pounded on the roof, the tic of hail meant going outside wasn't in the cards. I searched around, found flint and steel to start a fire, which I did, then turned up a long red coat that fell to mid thigh on me. The interior warmed quickly and I would have dosed the fire if not for the incessant rumblings of my stomach. The fourth trunk held their foodstuffs. It also contained a couple of pots, a pan, and flatware. Flour, salt, beans, and some spices that I had no clue about. I really questioned how good the sausage would be after all this time, but it didn't smell off at all. Oil, sugar cubes, what might have been lard rounded out what remained.

I set the copper pot out to collect water and put the cast iron skillet to the side of the stove to warm up. Flour, salt, and some water; I had dough for flatbread ready in a few minutes. Pot on to boil for the beans with some spices that smelled interesting. I let that cook for a while. I cut up a link of sausage to see if it was edible (Imagine my surprise that it turned out to be the case) and used the grease leftover in the pan to cook the bread.

I munched on the bread and meat while I waited on the beans. A sharp staccato beat on the roof over the dull drum of rain. I opened the book I'd picked up in the cave thinking to read while I ate. A note dropped to my lap as I opened the book.

If you're reading this then my summons worked. Please, save my family. They are all I have left. They will reward you for your help, but the spell book is yours to keep. It is little consolation I know for being torn from your world without return, but I did what I had to do. Forgive me if you can. My family will take what they need, the rest you may have.

May the Mother of Mysteries watch over you,

Osvaldo de Lima Montenegro

What the fuck?! Seriously, what the actual fuck? I zoned out of reality for a bit. My emotions ran the gamut and through a gauntlet of never-ending nightmare. My body went through the motions of living for the next few days after I returned to reality. I'd lost everything. I repeated the thought over and over. Until…

Wait, I'd already lost everything to that conniving- well, her. No children, no friends, no family. I'd miss modern conveniences but, magic! Even after growing up, that glimmer of hope remained a pale twinkle under the bright eye of reality. I grinned to the empty room and opened the spell book.

…choose carefully, young one, each choice limits future growth on the path of mastery. Refer back to the Novice Primer for Pathways of specialization.

I stopped there and searched the wagon. It wasn't a cursory search, I didn't just look around my immediate area. No, I looked under the beds and bedding; in and under the food chests; behind the walls and above the ceiling; until I'd rolled up the rugs and checked three quarters of the flooring. A false bottom that hung just above the rear axle contained seven thin primers.

Each covered evocation, summoning, conjugation, and divination within a Pathway. The first booklet described the different Pathways and gave some basic cantrips that introduced every Path, excepting necromancy, to give the starting novice a feel for their own natural inclination. Necromancy, the author described in a single sentence.

The foul art of the Necromancer is banned upon pain of death, without exoneration, pity, or mercy, throughout all civilized lands forevermore.

I didn't have a Primer for necromancy either; which I wasn't interested in if my memories of table-top games were anything to go by. The Sorcerer and Warlock Paths were also out due to the necessary enslavement of oneself or another sentient being.

Wizard and Mage sounded very similar. Wizards used the ambient mana in the environment to power their spells while the Mage increased the amount of mana their bodies could hold.

The Mage, though, were limited to the formula for a spell. Changes could cause explosive reactions with their mana and since they internalized their mana anything explosive was never good on, or near, the body.

The limiter on progress, I learned, was internal vs external mana usage. Very few practitioners could use both as one would have to split their mana channels, halving the efficiency of both Pathways. Mastery, or jack-of-all-trades, what did I want to do and be? Well, I didn't have to make a decision right now. I studied all the primers, maybe one pathway fit me better, physiologically.

I spent the days exploring the land around my wagon and my afternoons and nights studying the ways of magic. On the first morning, I laid the victims to rest. Using rusted pieces of metal and my hands, I dug graves for each of the family. The rest I threw into a shallow pit after removing any valuables, mainly tarnished copper and brass coins with a few silver pieces. Better than the nothing I started with.

My explorations uncovered horse remains and more fallen men in a line to a stream with a rotten bridge. A story played out here that I didn't have the skills to know. I looted the bodies and pushed the remains into a pile. These men didn't deserve anything better and they weren't close enough to my shelter to be a nuisance.

The stream, I noted, contained fish of sufficient size to help supplement the food in the wagon. A short walk away, the land dipped and a pond interrupted the stream. I noted the different plants within half a day's walk, especially the wild tea bushes. If tea here was anything like back home then this would be a major cash crop.

The spells, cantrips if I'm being honest, were the most difficult, but satisfying things I have ever worked on. Comprehend language I couldn't test yet, I hope it worked. The elemental spells and healing I picked up quickly. Knowledge of the body helped immensely and I could heal anything you would put a Band-Aid on. Moving a small amount of earth or air, and summoning water or fire, weren't very powerful but still: magic!

Concentration, I found, is key when performing any magic. Telekinesis worked my mind like barbells worked my arms, and the sensation was so odd, I almost quit using it. But, I convinced myself that, like any other muscle, it needed use, and exercised my mind daily. Teleportation had the potential to be the most useful and the most dangerous. I didn't have the power, or skills yet to move myself, but I could port small pebbles about ten meters away. No big deal on the surface, but I had the very important lesson of objects not being able to occupy the same space, reinforced for me.

I sat with my back to the fire, three pebbles orbiting around me as I practiced. I rubbed another rock between my thumb and forefinger, setting the teleport spell in my mind. I pictured it vanishing and reappearing outside the wagon. What I got was close. The unassuming rock merged with the wooden wall for an instant. Then both glowed a dull red and disappeared leaving a circular void seven centimeters in diameter in the wall. Letting in the rain. That mistake would drive me from the wilderness to civilization.

Chapter 2

After an exhausting search of the wagon I found a patch. One. I couldn't afford to mess up anymore and lose my shelter. I did find more letters that, while not addressed to me, were for the person summoned.

If the worst should come to pass and my family is already dead on your arrival, then the burden of continuing my House will fall upon you. I hereby affirm that,

I nearly dropped the parchment as my name filled in the blank spots left in the writing.

Daniel Hawthorne, is adopted into the Montenegro family as an heir. With all rights and responsibilities passing to Daniel, now Lord Montenegro, and those of his issue and choice.

May the Lady of Mysteries stand as witness and mark, Daniel del Montenegro, as befits the Duke of Montenegro.

I dropped the letter, will and testament, as black rings burned patterns into the back of my right hand. Two rings, one inside the other, formed an outer band while three interlocked rings fashioned a triangular shape in the center. The pain was excruciating. I blacked out for a moment. Then the agony disappeared as if it never began. But, the matte black brands remained. I ran a finger gingerly on the mark.

No pain nor indent. It was my skin, just a different color.

I picked the letter back up, but Osvaldo's signature and seal, the same one branding me, were the only thing left. On that page. The others covered land holdings, properties, and an account with the Bank of Lixa. The rest described the political situation before the summoning. Three other Duchies, Neves, Hoffmann, and Dalton, banded together to form the country of Tallinn. Montenegro and Koslov abstained until Dalton married a daughter into the Koslov family. Osvaldo suspected Dalton of the assassination of his House, but didn't have proof.

I spent the next two days immersed in the broad brush strokes of the political landscape. No one Duchy seemed to have prominence over another. Matter of fact, they balanced each other out, limiting the power any one House had over the others. Would they have split up the Montenegro holdings or left them to the Kingdom to hold in trust? One thing I knew for sure, no one would be happy to see me.

My new responsibilities wouldn't allow me to loiter around for long, but I only had a vague idea of where to go; I knew whatever passed for winter approached quickly. Cold weather travel in an unknown land was dangerous, to the point of suicide. I didn't even know what latitude my abductor placed me on. I'd stay and practice my magic to grow my personal power, then make my way to a town or city.

And so I spent the winter practicing what little I knew. Perfecting my skills and concentration. The air grew cold, though it never snowed; rain and sleet were common, I'd probably have died of exposure, if I tried to walk out of here. I worked for three months, exercising my mind and body. I didn't know the technological level of my new homeland, but not much beyond medieval Europe, if the dead bodies were anything to go by. The monetary system seemed based on precious metals shaped into coins. What would I run into next? Goblins and Elves?

The port and kinetic spells used external mana so I could progress them with training. I could now orbit five twenty pound rocks and teleport pebbles up to ten meters away. I could also make telekinetic shields that could stop rocks that I'd flung into the air. I did the best I could and now I wanted to leave.

I packed up what I could from the wagon, dressed in layers,

and threw on the red coat. Two makeshift packs on my back and a pouch on each hip, one held rocks and pebbles, and the other twelve silver and twenty-seven copper, all of various sizes. Ready to go, I locked up the wagon and restored the ward. I learned that trick from the pile of parchment. Which I'd also packed. I scratched at my wild unkempt beard.

I set out east, the forest still dark, but it lightened by the minute. For the next few days I camped in the open under stars I didn't recognize. I was a bit nervous to be honest. I didn't know what kind of reception I could expect or what form it would take. By the fourth day I found a road. Well, a dirt path about the width of my wagon with well worn ruts. The road wound between two hills, which is how I spotted it, parallel to my course. I thought for a moment and decided to take the road. What could go wrong?

Six days. It took six days of walking to meet another human being. That they wanted to rob me was beside the point. Call me wrong, but I missed social interaction with people.

"Looky here boys!" Said a short rugged man dressed in a brown leather jerkin. "What do we have here?"

Fine. I was wrong.

"Looks like a Mook boss!" Said another similarly short man. Though this one was missing several teeth.

Three other men stood up from around the fire that burned merrily on the side of the road. A boar rotated on a spit that made my stomach rumble loudly. They all laughed at the sound. None of these men topped a meter and a half in height.

"He's a tall one ain't he boss? Asked Toothless.

"I can see that," said Boss. He scratched his groin. "Alright Mook, take it all off and be on your way with no more than a story to tell."

I readied my shields and pulled out a handful of rocks. "And if I don't?"

"Well now, you won't have to worry about that belly of yours no more," Boss said with a sinister grin.

His intentions made clear, I teleported my stones one at a time into the heads of the bandits starting from the back.

I stared at Boss until the third body thudding into the road caught his attention. Toothless collapsed in front of him and Boss took two steps back before he too fell. I promptly vomited onto the dirt road. I'd never killed a person before and it hit me hard. I got myself under control by reminding myself that they would have done worse to me. One of the men already had his pants down before he died.

I buried them on the side of the road using my magic then took over their camp. While I didn't have much of an appetite there was no use in letting the boar go to waste.

I collected what little loot the bandits had, adding their coins to my purse, and left everything else. I didn't want to carry anything else.

The sun sat on the horizon when I could hear hoof beats pounding down the road. A few minutes later twelve people rode up to the bandit camp and milled around.

"They were right here I tell you," a statuesque woman dressed in pants and shirt with a blue vest said.

"I don't doubt you," a very muscular woman said. "But, the contract does not give us permission to chase after them in these woods."

I put my telekinetic shield up, just in case, and stood. "They-," I started to say, but something thumped into one of my shields, causing it to flare brightly. I looked down and saw a crossbow bolt at my feet, the tip bent.

"Stand down!" Muscles shouted. "Next one to loose a bolt without an order gets one up the ass!"

She turned to face me. "You, come here." When I didn't move fast enough she shouted, "Now!"

I really didn't want to kill anybody else so I stomped to the edge of the road, my hands in my pockets.

"What are you doing here?" Muscles asked.

"I was walking down the," I started to explain.

"I don't care," she shook her head. "Why. Are. You. Here?"

I sighed. "My camp is there," I pointed to it.

"Why?"

"Why not?" I threw back at her. It might cause some trouble, but my dander was up.

Her reddening face was a good barometer of trouble.

"Why," she took a deep breath. "Are you camped by where bandits have been sighted?"

"Because I no longer felt like traveling after I killed them."

"Wait, what?" She seemed confused. "Where are they then?"

"Behind you." I started to enjoy myself. Amanda always hated it when I got into a mood.

Muscles turned and looked at the freshly turned earth. She looked back at me. "I'm going to need some proof."

I nodded. "If you would remove your horses?"

She nodded and barked an order. The soldiers, that's what

they looked like, quickly moved away.

I pulled my marked hand out of my pockets then heard gasps from the group. I scratched at my unkempt beard.

Muscles swore under her breath. A few deft hand motions from me had the bodies exhumed.

Muscles briefly examined them and turned to me, her tone of voice much different. "You killed all five, Milord?"

I nodded. She closed her eyes and sighed. "And the goods, Milord? Have you claimed them?"

"Over there," I pointed them out. "And no, I don't claim them."

"Very good," she motioned, to the merchant I presumed.

"Will that be all…" I trailed off with a little shake of my head.

"Of course your Grace," she bowed with her arms straight along her torso. The other soldiers bowed as well when I passed them.

"Your Grace," I turned to the statuesque merchant. She folded at the waist, elbows bent, and hands behind her back. "If I might presume upon you?"

I frowned and asked, "What might be your presumption?"

"Would you allow us to camp near you?"

I thought for a moment. "And you are?"

"Forgive me your Grace. I am Safira Pereira, merchant of general goods in Olasa."

"Rise Safira," I said. "My camp is just over the rise," I gestured into the distance when she looked at me.

"Of course your Grace." She turned to the soldiers and shouted, "Load all this on the horses then follow."

The leader -I didn't know her rank- and two others followed Safira and I back to camp. I pointed out some logs, inviting them to sit, then sat myself by the fire. The boar had burned a bit on one side so I drew my knife and trimmed it up then cut long slices for my guests.

"You are traveling alone, your Grace?" Muscles asked.

"I am," I said and studied their reactions. They all had confused expressions in varying degrees of severity. "I'm new to the area and just passing through."

"Where do you go, Milord?" Safira asked.

"To Montenegro," surprise writ large upon their faces. "Does no one travel to the Duchy anymore?" I asked, exasperated.

"Some do, Milord," Muscles said cautiously. "Those without a House. But, nobles don't, especially not marked heirs."

"Ah," I said, and lifted my hand. "The time has come for me to claim my inheritance."

"You will walk the whole way?" she asked archly.

"No," I shook my head. "I will go to the nearest settlement and see about transportation from there."

"You should have an escort," she began, but Safira interrupted saying, "Finish the job you were hired to do first Captain Fallah.

Captain Fallah chuckled with a smirk, "We will Mistress Safira, but it doesn't hurt to set up the next business venture when the opportunity arises."

I didn't want to listen to them bicker back and forth so I coughed loudly to remind them I was still there.

"I might just take you up on that Captain." I nodded to her. "Consider this a working interview."

She sat back, her eyebrows raised, then lowered as she looked me up and down.

I shook my head. I ate my slice of pork then cut another, tough overcooked piece, but then again with wild boar, killing all the parasites held more importance than tenderness.

I continued slicing off portions until we all ate our fill. "Good night ladies. Captain, you have a watch schedule?"

"I do, Milord," her tone didn't say mind my own business, but her eyes certainly did.

As long as she got the job done I really didn't care. I set out my groundsheet, sleeping pallet, set some wards, then laid down. The eyes of dead men haunted my sleep.

Chapter 3

My eyes itched as I pried them open the next morning. An overfilled bladder had me rushing to a nearby tree. I probably shouldn't have been surprised at the admiring whistle from my right. I slowly turned my head to the right. The plain faced female soldier looked up, met my eyes, and smirked. She gave me a slow wink. I shook twice then tucked myself away. She pouted and walked away. I had to remind myself I couldn't.

People counted on me. People who didn't know I existed yet, but I was beholden to them. The people of my Duchy deserved a man, a Lord, who could keep it in his pants and not beget bastards that could muck-up the line of succession.

It helped, a little.

More awake now, I noticed the others breaking camp. Safira, in a green dress, smiled brightly as she noticed me looking.

"Good morning, your Grace."

"Good morning, Safira."

"Will you be joining us for the trip back to Olasa?"

I covered my mouth as I suddenly yawned. "If it won't be too much trouble," I finally managed to get out.

"Oh, it wouldn't be any trouble at all, Milord." She bobbed a low curtsey revealing a generous amount of cleavage.

I closed my eyes and took a deep breath. "Excellent," I smiled at her. Barking laughter interrupted my train of thought. I looked across the camp to see Captain Fallah slapping her knee. Plain face wiped her eyes next to her.

"What are those barbarians braying about now?" Safira asked.

"Someone got a show, and I guess it's funny."

"Your Grace?"

"Never mind," I shook my head. "If you will give me a few moments I'll be ready to travel."

Safira nodded with a frown, still watching the obnoxious

Captain.

By the time I had my things packed and ready to go, the rest of the company milled about on the road. Half the horses were packed with the merchant's goods while their riders held the reins. The rest formed up around the party with me and Safira walking in the middle. We all chatted amicably through the day though, in truth, I didn't pay much attention to what they said. By the time my stomach reminded me, and those close by, that I missed lunch the walls of Olasa appeared through a break in the trees.

Rough, brown stone blocks, made up the wall. At ten feet tall, they might slow down invaders, but not by very much. A pair of uniformed and unimpressive guards stood beside the gates, they didn't stop to check us, or ask our business in the town. I shrugged, none of my business, what they did or didn't do. The buildings in town were cut from the same stone as the wall; probably all from the same quarry.

I thought the red tiled roofs were nice. We entered a square on the main thoroughfare and Safira turned to me, "Your Grace, if I may?"

I nodded and she said, "If you need lodging, the Quiet Elf inn," she pointed to my right to a building that looked like all the others. "It's a good place, with clean rooms, and good food."

"Thank you Safira." I gave her a little bow. "That sounds like just what I need."

I walked over to the building hoping it was the one she pointed out. A small painted sign depicted a small elf on a mushroom either dead or asleep. It was difficult to tell for sure. I opened the door then went inside.

The room was cozy. Dark woods used on the walls and tables. Thick animal skins upholstered the chairs. Fireplaces on either end of the room burned merrily with people sprinkled about speaking quietly. Drinking tea. I stood shocked in front of the door, my expectations subverted, until someone hissed, "Close the door!"

I shook myself and gently pulled the door to. I looked around in vain trying to find the bar or someone for help. A soft voice to my left gave me hope, "Can I help you sir?"

A pretty blonde girl stood behind a podium or something. She couldn't have been much older than a teenager, but the severe look she gave me, disconcerted me for a moment. She shook her head minutely while raising her brow prompting me, "Ah, yes. Could I rent a room for the night?"

"I don't know. Can you?"

"Seriously?" My own brows challenged hers. "That's what you're going with? What are you? Twelve?"

She scowled and gestured to encompass my person. "Can

you pay for a room?"

I opened my mouth with a scathing retort on the tip of my tongue, but stopped. I could see her point. "I don't know. How much is it? A night's stay I mean."

She closed her eyes, "A copper Mark."

"Yeah, okay. Is that the small or big one?"

She sighed disgustedly, "The big one." She glanced around the room already done with the conversation.

I took the coin purse out of my pocket and peered inside. A little silver, the rest tarnished copper. I grabbed the smallest silver piece then set it on the podium.

She glanced down at it then back to me. Why is she acting like she's thirty? She drew herself up, "Do you require change, sir?"

After running me the riot act? "I do."

She harrumphed. An honest to god huff with the perfect amount of disdain. She impressed me despite myself. She handed me three copper Marks and a key. "Through the door," she waved imperiously at the far wall behind me. "Sixth door on your left."

I raised my hand and thumbed over my shoulder, "That way?"

Her haughty look disappeared. I could see her color visibly fade as she wobbled.

"Miss?" I can't lie, it felt good. Until I remembered I was intimidating a young woman. Real big of me.

She regained her composure quickly though. "If you would follow me, Milord?" She walked around me, plucking the key from my hand, "I will see you to your rooms."

I put my coin purse back into my pocket and hitched the pack more securely on my shoulder while trying to keep up. She walked with a weird sway. Hungry, tired, and more than a little out of sorts, I almost missed her small glance back at me. But, not her disappointed pout. Nope. Sorry for your luck.

"Here we are, Milord," she opened a door on the left side of the hall considerably further down than her directions before. "Will you require anything else?"

"Yes. I'd like a meal." She nodded. "Next I need a valet, or someone who can help get me things, whatever you might call them." Her brows furrowed. I barely stopped from rolling my eyes. "Fine. I need a bath, a way to get clothes, a haircut, and to find the Bank of Lixa so I can pay for all these things." I scrubbed my hand through my hair. "Oh, and someone who can explain customs, proper etiquette, manage estates, and I don't know what else; a Chamberlin or something."

Her jaw hung open as she stared at me until she visibly shook herself. "I will have a meal brought to you, Milord. And an attendant to see to your other needs." She curtseyed low, spun about then sped down the hallway.

I looked around the lushly appointed room. Plush brown rugs covered most of the wood floor complimenting the chocolate colored furnishings. The bed, chest-of-drawers, and two person table set were highly polished to a glossy shine. Of course the luxury stopped there since I'd have to bathe out of a bowl and shit in a pot.

A knock on the door saved me from that downward spiral. I had enough trouble 'going' in strange places as it was.

"Your dinner, Milord," the door girl announced as she led an older woman carrying a heavily laden, cloth covered tray. She swept into the room, then gestured the woman to the table. The woman wasn't ugly, but there's probably a reason the girl brought her, instead of someone else. "Will there be anything else, my Lord?" the girl simpered.

"Other," I crossed my arms. "Than what I've asked for, you mean?"

"Umm," she toyed with a lock of hair. "Yes?"

"No." I raised my chin, "That will be all."

Her crestfallen look did not sway me. "Very good, Milord."

I gestured towards the door and noticed the woman smirk. Apparently, fresh from the kitchen, as the front of her white shirt was wet and quite see-through. I met her eyes, she winked at me. I kept the sneer off my face, barely.

And while I like tits, I wasn't in a receptive mood. No, tired, hungry, and still blaming women in general for my broken heart, I didn't appreciate the come-on. Intellectually, I know that makes no sense, but it's how I felt. Deal with it. I have to. Besides, I have responsibilities, while a quick dalliance might sound like fun, I don't know what all the ramifications might be to something like that. Bastards have been known to cause problems within lines of succession.

"That will be all for now ladies." I pulled out a chair. "Thank you."

I removed the napkin and out of habit put it in my lap. The roast chicken smelled divine. I was surprised to see potatoes, but they were synonymous with human cuisine for hundreds of years. That meant it wasn't mind blowing for me. It did raise the question of whether they were native, or if they were brought here by a traveler like me, somehow.

I dug into the food and several minutes later a light cough reminded me the serving woman still stood there. I plucked up my napkin then dabbed my lips.

"Yes?" I asked while wiping my hands.

"My Lord, will you require anything else?"

"What else?" I stopped myself. "As a matter of fact, I would like a bath." She slowly touched her top lip with her tongue.

"Are there facilities for that or will you have to drag in some sort of contraption?"

The poor woman looked lost for words. She might have answered, but then the door girl walked in with an older man.

He looked around then said to the girl, "Adequate, I suppose." He pointed to the woman. "Out. His grace will properly observe propriety."

He sounded even more pompous than I did; I loved it. He closed the door on the woman's backside, she gave a muffled squeak as the door smacked her, looking at me the entire time.

"Interesting," he said softly then cleared his throat. "I am Anton Kos, your Grace." He bowed low at the waist. "And I am applying to be your personal Steward." He rose smoothly. "And I am quite expensive."

He openly gazed upon the room with a slight sneer. "But, my loyalty is absolute. I am qualified to see to all your basic needs, and I am quite knowledgeable in many different aspects, so as to help procure anything else you might require."

"That sounds excellent Mr. Kos," I wiped my hands again then grabbed my travel pack to dig out my letters. I quickly found my bank statement of ownership and handed it to him.

"Will this account still be accessible?" I asked.

"It should never expire as the bank will invest any funds left in the account," Anton looked up in thought. "The bank of Lixa is still in operation but," he held his finger up. "They are partnered with the Royal Bank. You would not be able to withdraw all monies owed to you, but having enough for expenses should not be a problem."

"Good. Then tomorrow morning we will go secure my funds. Then see to a tailor and a barber," Anton nodded along at every word. "I asked for a bath previously but…"

Anton stood up straight then bowed with his arms straight with his torso. "I will see to it your Grace." He paused for a moment, "Will there be anything else my Lord?"

"I'm sure there are details that I don't know about or have missed. If you think something is important then please schedule it in for tomorrow," I nodded to him.

"Very good, Milord," he backed to the door. "I will see to everything."

I went back to my meal after Anton closed the door. As I ate, I thought about the situations I might have to endure. This was going to be more difficult than I initially thought if adult women were going to throw themselves at me. I wasn't celibate, or a virgin. But, to show honor my position, and the family I'd been adopted into, then I needed to be very careful about my associations.

Not long after I'd finished eating, Anton knocked and let himself into the room. "Your Grace, the facilities are ready for your use. A barber will be there at your discretion," he motioned to the door with a bow.

"Thank you Mr. Kos," I stood and placed the napkin on the plate. "If you would be so good as to show me the way?"

"Of course my Lord," he stood and walked into the hall. "This way, if you please."

Anton led me down the hallway towards the back to the building. A stone archway framed a beaded curtain, and the floor transitioned abruptly from carpet to flagstone. It looked like someone knocked out part of a wall, then started building in a different material. The effect jarred me, but not enough to care; It was only an aesthetic.

We crossed the small entrance room, to another beaded curtain in an archway, offset from the other enough that one could not see into the large bathroom by happenstance. At the far end of the room, two in-ground tiled pools steamed into the cool air. To the left, stone cubbies stood along the wall, presumably to hold a customer's belongings. Along the wall to the right, were shower stalls that while open, gave a modicum of privacy from the wooden sides. Further down, were three padded slabs reminiscent of a massage table. Two men waited at attention by the tables.

Anton stepped to the side and gestured to the cubbies. "Your Grace, if you will, please place your clothes here. Then, as is the custom," he eyed me carefully. "One uses the shower first, dries off, then continues on to the masseur. Oils and scents are applied in a relaxing massage. Afterwards, the barber will see to your haircut and shave." I nodded along. "Then a relaxing soak finishes the experience."

I pulled my coin purse out of my pocket and handed it to him. "Very good Mr. Kos," I moved to the cubbies and disrobed. "But, have them just trim my beard. I've grown attached to it." I didn't have a problem being naked in a locker room, and this wasn't much different.

I showered quickly, then made my way to the massage table. Though the massage experience was great, it felt a little awkward on my end. I don't know how the masseur felt, but I'm pretty sure my boner made everyone uncomfortable. I'm not attracted to guys, but I didn't expect, or anticipate that he was going to oil everywhere, so thoroughly. I mean everywhere. I submerged fully into the hot water, gratefully hiding my shame with my eyes closed.

The surface of the pool glimmered like a kaleidoscope, with a simmering rainbow of colors from the oils rubbed into my skin. Deciding to go to bed after my eyes grew too heavy, I left the pool, then dried off.

The others had already left, save Anton, who read a book by the doorway. He stood with alacrity, the book snapping shut, and said, "Ready, my Lord?"

"I am, Mr. Kos, thank you."

I dressed quickly and gathered the rest of my belongings, then followed Anton to my room. He bade me wait before opening the door and sticking his head inside. A few moments later, after making sure of a clear room, he gave me a bow and said, "Good night your Grace."

"Thank you Mr. Kos," I said as I entered the room. "And to you as well."

He drew the door shut, finally alone I disrobed, then collapsed into bed, and knew no more.

Chapter 4

A light tapping woke me and I shouted, "Just a moment!" I dressed quickly then opened the door.

"Your Grace," Anton said as he bowed low. "The tailor is scheduled to fit you in an hour before you break your fast, then you have a meeting with the Bank manager an hour before lunch. If that pleases my Lord?"

"Very good Mr. Kos," I nodded to him. "Thank you."

The tailor, an unattractive, rail thin, older woman who was all business. Her long thin nose twitched with every measurement taken. Her assistant, so equally unattractive she had to be a relative, wrote down everything the tailor, Ms. Lidmila Stedry, said with her dry raspy voice. She smacked her lips before and after every word. The moist clicks grated on my every nerve.

Thankfully, Mr. Kos handled all interactions with the woman so I could keep my irritation hidden. He handed her some coins, she shook her head, he handed her some more then scowled at her. She started to shake her head again, but he pointed his finger at her, and she acquiesced with a defeated nod. Anton nodded as well, and gestured to the door.

Anton stepped up beside me and said, "Proper clothing will be delivered before your meeting at the bank, my Lord."

"Excellent Mr. Kos," I nodded. "Please have something to eat delivered while I wait."

"Very good, Milord."

I grabbed my spell book from my pack and sat at the table to study before my next appointment. I focused on the Arcane arts, teleportation and telekinesis more specifically, and was neutral to the other elements. So far, I haven't been able to manifest Arcane energy enough to make a bolt or missile, but I had high hopes. A better barrier of some kind was also one of my goals. Once I chose an Element, say fire, then its opposition to water would close to me. Every Element had its pluses and minuses. Air and Water were necessary for life, but Earth could do a lot of good for the greater populace. Fire, of course, is destructive, and a force multiplier. But, then Water would be lost to me.

I practiced while I read, five pebbles orbited around me, and one would bounce when I tapped my finger on the table. My goal, to develop mental control before power, was taxing, but nothing worth doing is ever easy.

A light tapping broke my focus and my rock collection fell around me. Some bouncing off the table.

Anton stood in the doorway, and cleared his throat then said, "Your Grace, your clothes are here." He looked at the scattered stones quizzically for a moment then bowed. A moment later he gestured for the tailor's assistant to enter the room.

She came in with two cloth garment bags held high. They were long and plain, but heavy duty, perfect for transporting new clothes.

She laid them out on the bed, "Will that be all, my Lord?"

I nodded and gestured to Anton.

He dug into his purse, handed something to her, and gestured her out. Anton closed the door then asked, "Will you require help, Milord?"

"No, Mr. Kos, that will be all. Thank you."

"Very good, Milord," he said and left the room.

I went to the bed and inspected my new clothes. Two identical outfits in black and silver trim, my House colors. Socks, pants, shirt with laces at the neck, and mage robes. I wanted a large silver rose embroidered on the back, but it would have taken too much time. So instead I had a Phoenix on each cuff and over the heart. I changed quickly and pulled the robe over my head, when a knock sounded at the door again. "Enter," I said.

Anton came in, then bowed his head. "It is time for your meeting at the bank."

I nodded, straightened my robe, and with a mental nudge collected the rocks and slipped them into a small brown leather bag, then sat that down on the table. I closed my spell book, then put it into my robe pocket.

"Very well, Mr. Kos," I motioned to him. "Please lead the way."

He bowed at the waist, " Of course, Milord."

Anton led me out of the Inn and into the busy street. We stayed to the side to avoid, not only the horses and the occasional carriage, but the droppings left behind. After months by myself, the crowd around me was both nice, and disconcerting at the same time. I'd been through worse at the airport, so I dealt with the discomfort.

We stayed on the major thoroughfares, not taking any shortcuts through alleyways, which I thought smart. That always seemed like something a dumb character in a novel would do. Go out of sight in a strange city to cut a few minutes off of travel time. I patted my waist, then noticed my pouch of rocks wasn't there. I just shook my head.

After ten minutes of walking, we made it to the bank without any problems. The structure stood alone on the corner in the middle of Olasa. The brown stone blocks of the building blended in with the rest of Olasa, though the architecture was nicer. The door featured an archway, with carved gargoyles crouched on either side, guarding the entrance.

The interior was bright and airy, with white marble floors and light colored furniture. Sconces gave off a steady soft glow. I walked through, amazed by the utility of the magic used here. It seemed the use of magic was a sign of wealth and power. Anton led me to the right, towards a large desk that I would normally associate with the information desk or greeting area of any large business.

"Anton Kos," he began our introduction. "And his Grace, Lord Montenegro," he said to a well dressed, spindly, hatchet faced man. "We are here by appointment."

"Of course, my Lords," the man said in a surprisingly deep voice. "If it pleases you to follow me?" His enormous Adam's apple continued to bob well after he finished speaking.

He led us off further to the right side of the building, up a set of stairs, to a corner office. Our guide lifted a trembling hand to knock on what would presumably be, the manager's door. Sweat marked the back of his shirt and underarms as he knocked a second time. Anton stood comfortably at ease. My attention diverted as the door opened.

Our guide stood off to the side and bowed us through the door. Looked like he wouldn't be joining us. The view through the windows directly ahead looked out over the city center square. Hundreds of people walked around going about their daily lives. None of the noise or smells reached us here. I liked it.

Someone coughed and I turned to my right. Anton had continued on, as I looked out the window, and stood in front of a large, if simple, desk. A rotund porcine looking woman sat with her thick fingers tapping on the desktop. Two men flanked her on either side. And while neither were intimidating, they both gave off a looming air. The woman did not rise as I stopped at the chairs in front of the desk.

She waved a hand and said magnanimously, "Have a seat," in a high pitched voice. "My name is, Tsveta Wolinsk," she held out her heavy, ring laden hand for me to kiss.

I looked at Anton out of the corner of my eye. His eyes were wide and his gaze darted around the room.

I took that moment to loosen the strings on my purse and set six coppers floating and orbiting around me. Any port in a storm. Without touching the odious woman I pulled out a chair and sat without invitation.

"Hmmm, you seem to labor under the misapprehension," she gestured to the bouncers then let her hand drop. "That you have power here."

Anton stumbled back as the men stalked around the table towards me. Two of my copper coins disappeared and the men stiffened before falling to the floor.

"No," I said calmly. "I don't think I have."

It frightened me a little, the simplicity of killing. They would have hurt me badly at the very least, and I felt only a twinge of conscience, easily shrugged off. Using coins was fitting in a way. There should be a cost to killing.

Tsveta sat pale and sweaty. "What have you done? My poor boys!" Her lip quivered. "How could you?"

I leaned back and crossed my right leg over my knee. "To business shall we?" I asked then glanced at Anton. "Mr. Kos, if you will?"

Anton licked his lips and a sheen of sweat betrayed his nervousness. "Yes. Of course My Lord," he said with a slight strain in his voice.

His throat bobbed and he exhaled slowly. "Miss Wolinsk," Anton's voice firmed and strengthened as he continued. "As I informed you before: his Grace, Lord Montenegro, wishes to make a withdrawal of funds."

Her gaze flitted between the both of us before settling on Anton. "How," she stopped and licked her fleshy lips. "How much will, his Grace, require?"

Anton looked at me. This wasn't something that we had discussed. My goal was to examine the records and get an idea of my financial standings in the world.

"All of it," I said.

Tsveta wiped her sweaty palms on the pleats of her dress. "We," her voice broke and her face scrunched up. A tear fell from the corner of her eye. "We don't have that much here, your Grace."

I looked at Anton and said, "Records."

"Of course your Grace," he said and held out his hand to her. "The statements please."

She wiped her hands once again, opened a drawer, and thrust a thick file into his hand. Anton presented the folder to me. I accepted and then opened it. I blinked several times.

Royal Bank of Tallinn

Account balance:

122 trade bars: gold Bullion

One hundred thousand Crowns each

531 trade bars: gold Heart

One thousand Crowns each

472 trade bars: silver Finger

One hundred Crowns each

8,775,323 gold Crowns

7,983,245 silver Marks

75,461 copper Pennies

12 th day of Jeul, 3145

"What is today's date?" I asked without looking up.

"Milord, it is the 23 rd of Augg," Anton said.

"Very well," I flipped the pages around of the different holdings, leases, and lands that held no meaning for me. I glanced up at Tsveta, "Then how much of my capital is your branch able to release today?"

Tsveta swallowed aloud. "We keep twenty gold Hearts as a reserve and ten thousand in Crowns and Marks. Double that in Pennies and Quarters," she said then added, "Your Grace."

I frowned at her. "How many branches of the Royal Bank are there?"

I didn't think it was possible, but she went even more pallid. "Twenty, your Grace."

"And if all branches keep a similar Reserve, there is no way for me to withdraw my funds without collapsing the Royal Bank," I leaned back in my chair and steepled my hands.

"I, umm, I cannot speak to that, your Grace."

"Would I be correct in that you have a way to communicate with someone who can, 'speak to that?'" I asked, scratching at my beard.

"Yes my Lord," she nodded vigorously, happy to pass this problem on to someone else.

"Then let us do that," I said with a smile.

It took an hour of various officials passing the buck around before I spoke with what in my world would be the CEO of the bank, a baroness, and got down to business.

"Greetings to you, your Grace," a light feminine voice said from the muted glowing stone on Tsveta's desk. "And, if I may, congratulations on your elevation as well."

"Thank you, my Lady," I said with lukewarm cordially. I didn't need to be rude, yet. But, I wasn't the one who needed to find a solution that didn't beggar this new Kingdom.

The stone's glow dimmed in the lengthening silence then the light pulsed, "How can we make this right, your Grace?"

A good thing she couldn't see me smile.

Four hours later, I owned seventy percent of the Royal Bank of Tallinn. Sizable amounts of Bullion and coinage were in route to my—personal—bank in Montenegro, guaranteed and secured by the Royal Bank, for delivery. It cost me twelve million Crowns, but I expected to earn that back in a few years, in fees, interest, and loans to the Kingdom. Surprisingly, or maybe not, those with magical gifts could use something like travelers checks, though they called them Bank Notes.

The Notes were in denominations of ten, one hundred, and one thousand Crowns. I could "sign" them by channeling my personal mana into the designated spot on the check. They could get wet, dirty, or torn and so long as the mana seal was intact they would be usable tender. Thick wedges of money clipped Notes weighted down the pockets of my robe on both sides.

Chapter 5

The light was fading as we left with heavy purses, and I felt great. This afternoon's interactions reminded me of my company on Earth. I loved going to work everyday and missed the give and take of negotiations. The battle with a competent opponent and coming out on top.

So, with a light heart, I tossed a few Marks to a street urchin on the corner. The scamp ran off as a crowd of filthy children suddenly surrounded us. Anton looked at me as if I'd lost my mind.

I drew on my power and lit up the twilight on the street. A new and harmless trick I learned. The children paused in fear then bolted. But, not before I saw a young man glow in response. He stared down at his shaking hands in astonishment and terror.

I called out to him, "You there!" He looked up at me. I held out a shiny gold Crown. "Come here, lad."

Anton asked, "My Lord?"

"Mr. Kos," I said as I beckoned the young man to me, as though he was a frightened animal. "I want to hire this young man. And an extra," and I made sure to raise my voice. "Crown for him to meet us at the inn for dinner."

"Are you sure, Milord?" Anton's face scrunched up in confusion.

I laughed, "Yes, Mr. Kos. And no I haven't lost my mind." I looked at Anton soberly. "This discussion is not suitable to have in the street."

Anton whipped his head around to look at the young man, then back and forth several times. A look of horror dawned on his face.

I laughed again, louder this time. "No, Mother of Mysteries, no. Not that!" I nearly choked myself with laughter, and tears streamed from my eyes.

Anton's face paled, turned red, then paled again. His mouth opened and closed, but no sound emerged.

He finally stuttered out, "My Lord, I, I…"

I wiped my eyes and said, "I will explain in due course. Will you trust me?"

Anton took a deep breath, "Of course, Milord. My apologies."

"Very good, Mr. Kos," I slapped him on the shoulder. "Give him directions and this coin please."

"Right away, Milord!" Anton ran over to the boy and began instructing him.

A few minutes later with the youth in tow, we made our way back towards the inn.

"Yur, Grace. Umm, what," the filthy teen stuttered and tripped over his tongue.

"What is your name? And how old are you?" I asked.

"Drazan, my Lord. Twenty, last winter." He bit his tongue to stop from rambling, but his eyes darted this way and that, possibly looking for danger or escape. "Drazan Lenart, but my friends call me Dazz."

"Well Dazz, you seem to have an unusual talent," I said calmly. "I'd like to talk to you over dinner about a job." I hoped to alleviate his fears and keep him from bolting.

"Umm, what kind of job, Milord?" His eyes stopped darting around and locked in on my face, though he still looked panicked.

"In all fairness," I said, looking him in the eye. "I want your loyalty," I gestured to placate him. "I know. But, earning and keeping your trust starts now." I took a deep breath. "I want you to be a retainer for the Montenegro family." I shook my head as he inhaled to speak. "Not as a servant so to speak, serving meals and the like. But, what you would do, would be determined by your talents."

He stumbled a bit, but recovered quickly. "My Lord, I would be honored to serve your family," he stopped and bowed low in gratitude. Which revealed the group of guards trotting up behind us.

"Excellent!" I turned to Anton, hiding the passing of my new purses, "Take Dazz to the inn, get him cleaned up, then bail me out of whatever passes as a jail here." The guards seemed to only have eyes for me.

Anton hid my fortune deftly and grabbed Dazz by the arm. He turned them both to face the guards from behind me.

They stopped a couple of meters away and I raised my marked hand towards them. "Good evening gentlemen," I greeted. "What can I do for you?"

"Your, umm, lordship," the lead guard didn't look sure of himself as he stared at my hand. "We would like to, umm, ask you to come with us," he looked back at his fellows for support that wasn't there as they all looked everywhere, but at him or me.

"To what might I owe the pleasure of your company?" I asked. It didn't seem like a shakedown, at least not anymore.

"Umm, what, Milord?" The guard looked confused.

"I am rather busy and have a dinner meeting to attend," I began. "Why do you need me to go with you?" I shook my head. "Is something wrong?"

"Oh," he shook himself. "No, Milord. Nothing is wrong." He wiped sweat from his brow. "But, the city lord, he, uh, heard about yourself. And wanted to talk to you."

"Very well," the guards visibly deflated. "But, I will require an escort for the evening to and from this unscheduled meeting." The lead guard tensed. "You gentlemen will be available."

"Umm, of course your Grace," he said with a sigh.

They escorted me back, passed the bank, to an opulent manor with wide grounds surrounding the estate. Trimmed lawns were spotted with manicured trees, all surrounded by a meter tall cast-iron fence. The guards led me to the stone gatehouse set to the right of the decorative gate. It wouldn't stop an attack, but it was very pretty.

"Umm, here we are, Milord," the lead guard said before stopping before the checkpoint.

"What is your rank, guardsmen?" I asked while putting my hand into my pocket feeling for the octagonal shape of gold Crowns.

"Well, Sergeant. If it pleases, Milord," the Sergeant said confused.

I found three Crowns and pulled them out. "I want an escort and unquestioned obedience," I said, showing them the coins.

"Of course, your Grace. It would be our greatest honor," the Sergeant said and bowed along with his men.

"Excellent," I said and handed over the coins. "First, your main concern is to protect me. You don't answer questions and you obey only me. You are now under the protection of Duke Montenegro." I gave each man a firm look into their eyes as I spoke. "Our goal is to go to this meeting and get it over with as quickly as possible."

I stepped up to the Sergeant, "I might have to stay for dinner, but food will be provided for you afterwards." The men behind the Sergeant looked let down. "Quality food, not whatever you normally get." They perked up a little. "I don't know this lord nor his staff. I don't want you to risk being compromised while we are there."

"Umm, compromised, Milord?" One of the men asked.

"Poisoned or intoxicated," I said firmly. "I don't want to slander this Lord's good name, but worse things have been known to happen in politics."

The Sergeant and guards nodded knowingly.

"So, accept no gifts—food or otherwise—and do not answer questions," they nodded along with me.

"Follow my orders as they are given, and more Crowns will be yours. Any questions?"

The Sergeant and I looked around, but the men simply shook their heads. "Excellent! Follow me," I said as we continued on to the guard house. The people around the, what could be more honestly attributed as, a shack milled around with the boredom of repetition. No one in their right mind would assault the city Lord.

"Halt!" One of the city Lord's men shouted. "Who goes there and what's yer business?"

I nodded to the Sergeant and he stepped forward and asked. "Max, that you?" He didn't wait for a reply and continued, "I'm

Sergeant Jur Koval, commanded to invite and escort His Grace, Duke Montenegro, to the manor of the City Lord, Baron Miros Vlaeva, who issued the command."

"How's do I know yer tellin' the truth?" The guard asked suspiciously.

I turned to the Sergeant, Jur, and said loudly, "Sergeant Jur, I am a busy man and they have interrupted my current business to be here. We leave in sixty seconds."

A runner from the manor slid on the gravel drive and crashed into the ornate gates. He huffed and puffed, clearly out of breath, but managed to get out, "Let. Them in." He took several deep breaths.

"Now." Then he collapsed onto the gravel.

The guard that might, or might not, be Max shouted out orders to open the gate. Clanks echoed out from the guard house and I could picture someone cranking a windlass as fast as they could. The gate ponderously slammed open and I felt the vibration through my feet when the gate hit the stops.

Max, a twenty-something young man with brown hair, came up to us and bowed. "My Lord, if it pleases you, the Baron awaits your pleasure," he said, all traces of his former accent gone.

I nodded and gestured for the guards to lead the way. My new detail formed up around me as we continued on to the manor house. The driveway was so long it took us a few minutes to get to the front door. We were greeted by the servants, lined up with whom, I guess, was the Baron and Baroness standing in front of them. A young woman stood beside the nobles. The staff all wore matching yellow tunics with four petal rose heraldry sewn onto the left breast.

The lord and lady matched in soft blue. A tunic for him and a dress, or maybe gown would be closer, for her. The young lady definitely wore a gown. Low cut at the bust and cinched at the waist; the sleeves flared and hid most of her hands. The red of the dress contrasted nicely with her wide silver belt. None of them looked happy.

One of the staff walked out of the line and approached. My guards lined up behind me. "Your Grace, might I introduce you to my Lord, Baron and Baroness Vlaeva, and their cousin Lady Tuga Banich," he said with a flourishing bow.

I nodded my head respectfully. Sergeant Jur made to step forward, but stopped when I motioned him back. "My Lord and Ladies, thank you for your gracious invitation. It seems you have caught me at a disadvantage, as my carriage is undergoing repairs," I lied. In my defense, I did plan on buying a carriage. And who knew if it needed repairs? But, by walking, I showed weakness. That I lie on the same level as all of the other peasants. It was bullshit, but opinions shaped perception, and if they perceived weakness, then I was in danger. So I lied.

"That is most unfortunate," the Baroness Vlaeva said. Her voice, mellow and smooth, didn't have the same lilt that the natives did, though it was the same language my spell translated. I only stopped empowering that spell when I slept. The people of the city sounded Eastern European, but the Baroness' accent hinted at a Frankish influence.

"Your Grace," she continued. "Let us not keep you out in the night air, please, won't you come in?"

"I would be delighted, my Lady," I said.

She looked over my shoulder, "Have you misplaced your chaperone?" She asked with a glint in her eye.

I narrowed my eyes at her. "He is looking to finish up some business on my behalf, that I was in the middle of when," I paused and looked back at Jur. "I accepted your invitation." I looked back at her and smiled. "These fine gentlemen have pledged to watch over me and guarantee my behavior."

The glint in her eye grew as her smile did. Someone coughed and she at least had the decency to look embarrassed. I didn't believe it for a second. She looked down demurely for a moment then hooked her elbow to mine and led me into the manor.

"We were about to sit down for dinner, my Lord. Would you honor our home by joining us?" She asked as we passed through the double doors, into a small sitting room, and on into a hallway with scenic paintings. Her fingers stroked my arm and I pretended not to notice.

"I would be delighted," I said, then gestured behind me. "I will unfortunately have to have a couple of my chaperones with me." I looked at her from the corner of my eye as she glanced up at me sharply. "That won't be a problem will it?"

"Of course not, your Grace," she said with a pout. "Whatever you require can be arranged." Her emphasis did not go unnoticed.

"Yes your Grace, we would be honored for you to join our family dinner," The Baron said drolly. He seemed used to his wife's antics.

We entered a formal dining room with a long light wood table. It sat twelve comfortably, but only four settings were set out at the far end. The Baroness patted my arm before she released me and made her way to the left of the head of the table. The Baron gestured to the seat to his right and bade me sit. The cousin sat to my right. Thankfully the table was wide enough that I didn't have to worry about the Baroness playing footsie with me.

Servants filled our glasses with a light white wine after we were seated. We made small talk about the weather for a few minutes before the first course of a summer salad arrived. It seemed we all had our own personal waiters. Mine stood by the wall with the Sergeant and one of his men.

I waited until the other nobles began eating before I selected the same style fork they did. My upbringing readied me for formal dining in the European style and my hosts seemed to follow suit.

The Baroness kept the subjects light as we talked. The weather, how our day went, and similar topics. She continued in this way through the hors d'oeuvre, small squares of flat bread with creamed mushroom. They were light and savory with a hint of basil.

After those dishes were removed, the Baron asked me, "So what brings you to our little backwater of Olasa, your Grace?"

Everyone in the room quieted and I looked around. The Baron clapped his hands then said, "Please, forgive them. We do not often have guests, and often treat the servants as family."

He bowed while seated and said, "They mean no offense."

I waved away his apology, "No offense taken, my Lord." I took a sip of wine. "Just passing through on my way home."

The Baron nodded, "I heard there was some trouble at the

Royal Bank today; would you know anything about this?"

"About how Ms. Wolinsk tried to strong arm me out of my coin?" I asked with a frown.

He frowned back, "She was reported to be nearly hysterical. If I may, what happened?"

I gave him my side of the story minus my account information.

"Truly, Milord?" Lady Tuga asked. "You are a Magic-user?" She leaned closer to me and the Baroness glanced at her husband before she sat back pouting.

"Well, I am still new to my power," I said. "But, I am learning."

The Baron smiled and asked, "Are you by chance betrothed, your Grace?"

I needed to nip this in the bud as soon as possible. I'm sure Tuga was a lovely person, but my future wife would also be a political marriage alliance. And I would hazard a guess that the Banich family did not have the political clout that would make them normally eligible for such a union. Though, it would be a masterful political coup for the Baron.

"Negotiations are still ongoing, but nothing is official yet," I said with a calm I did not feel. "Do you have someone in mind?" I pointedly did not look at Tuga.

He didn't get the hint. "Well, my Lord, my cousin Lady Tuga is currently available," he said and pointed her out.

I looked into her hope filled brown eyes and dashed her aspirations. "Have her Proctor or representative send it to my Chancellor and," I turned back to the Baron. "The negotiations can begin."

"Oh, you don't handle matters yourself, my Lord?" The Baroness asked archly.

I glanced over to her then back to the Baron. "No, my union will be one of politics, not of love. So needs must, I'm afraid."

The Baron nodded in commiseration, "Yes, my Lord, we all must make sacrifices for family at times like these. Even to form a family." He tapped the table and servants rushed in to place covered plates in front of us. "And with a magical bloodline, your list of eligible women will inevitably be small."

The servants removed the covers with a flourish, revealing a gravy soaked roast on mashed potatoes with multi-hued carrots on the side.

"Yes," said the Baroness with a smirk. "You might have to wait for years before your wedding night."

"Too right, my Lady," I replied. "I will not have bastards to muck up the lines of inheritance."

Tuga gasped and the Baroness covered her mouth with her

hand. A bit excessive to my sensibilities, but it is a different culture.

"Your Grace," the Baron started carefully. "Does not Montenegro's line of inheritance follow the mother's bloodline?"

I scratched my beard while I thought carefully, for a long moment, on how to present myself without showing weakness, or ignorance. "It has to do with the genealogical markers that are inherent," I lifted my hand. "To the magic, signifying all of my progeny, especially my heir, to bear the same markers." I looked at the Baron pointedly. "Does that alleviate your concern, my Lord?"

"Yes, quite," He took a long gulp of wine.

We finished the rest of the meal in tense silence. Lady Tuga stared at the tablecloth, Baroness Vlaeva handed out coy glances as though they were candy, and the Baron pointedly ignored everyone else. I particularly enjoyed the chocolate pudding covered with whipped cream for dessert. Knowing there was chocolate in this world, eased a tension I didn't know I had.

I wanted to get back to the inn so I stood, my waiter quickly pulled out my chair, and I said, "My Lord and Ladies, thank you for your gracious hospitality and wonderful meal," I tilted my head down more than I had previously. "But, I really must attend to some pressing matters of importance."

I stepped to the side away from the table and looked at the Sergeant. He nodded his understanding. "I bid you all a good evening."

One of the Vlaeva servants rushed ahead of me to see us out. The Baroness half stood, but sat abruptly with a sour look on her face. The Baron and his cousin didn't bother looking up from their wine.

We were soon headed up the driveway, the crunch of gravel loud in the night air. Putting on airs and playing a pompous aristocrat was exhausting. The Sergeant's stomach grumbled its own complaints.

Okay, I didn't have it that bad, and… Who was I kidding? I had it great!

So, with a smile, I turned my head to Sergeant Jur and said, "You and your men did an excellent job, Sergeant." They formed up around me as we turned to walk up the cobblestone street.

"Now, who knows how to get to the Quiet Elf inn?"

The rest of the journey through the city was uneventful. After entering the inn, I told the girl, the same one that checked me in, "Give Sergeant Jur and his men whatever they wanted to eat." I turned away, took two steps, then turned back and said,

"Oh, and they drink on my tab tonight." I looked at the men, "Enjoy yourselves gentlemen." I could still hear them cheering until I closed my room door.

Mr. Kos greeted me almost immediately. "My Lord, you are safe!"

"Thank you, Mr. Kos." I looked at the teen boy getting up from my table. "How are you lad? Good?"

He nodded vigorously.

"Excellent. Please, sit."

He sat.

"Can I have something brought for you?"

He shook his head.

"Have you the ability to speak?" I asked.

He nodded.

"Very well," I said, then looked at Anton and asked, "Would you see to having someone bring us a bottle of wine and some juice?"

"Right away, Milord," Anton said and hurried out the door.

I walked over to Drazan and said, "To explain quickly, you can learn magic. My offer is simple. I train you, and then you work for my family for no less than ten years. What do you say?"

"My Lord, I would be honored to serve," Dazz bowed low. "I vow to serve your Grace, and the Montenegro family, for life or until released from service. May the Mother of Mysteries hear and mark my Vow."

He grunted and gripped his left wrist. A silver Phoenix etched itself into the skin on the back of his left hand. Anton's gasp revealed his presence and he quickly slammed the door shut.

Anton Kos knelt beside Dazz and offered up his own service, "Your Grace, I humbly ask to be sworn into your service."

I didn't understand, so I asked, "Why would you want to swear such an oath?"

"My Lord, you have carried yourself with honor," Anton said with his head bowed. "You will not be pushed around, and." He paused for a moment, "If I am honest; I wish to ride your coattails to greatness."

I smiled even though he couldn't see it. "I understand self-interest very well. Mr. Kos, will you take service to me and my family? Will you serve in the capacity of your talents, and otherwise, if the need arises?"

Anton raised his head and spoke in a clear voice, "I vow to serve your Grace, and the Montenegro family, for life or until released from service. May the Mother of Mysteries hear and mark me."

Anton grunted as the silver Phoenix marked his left hand.

"Thank you both for the trust you have displayed. I will endeavor to always be worthy of the faith you have placed in me," I said.

I reached out to Anton and grasped his shoulder, "You should know how I became the Duke of Montenegro."

And so I told them of my origins. Their reactions were lukewarm at best.

"Neither of you seem surprised," I said while eyeing them suspiciously.

They looked at one another and Dazz nodded to Anton. Mr. Kos looked at me and shrugged, "The Mother of Mysteries controls the magnificence of magic and is magnanimous in her mercy."

"Did you just," my face scrunched up involuntarily. "Quote scripture at me?"

"Yes my Lord," Anton said. "That is the beginning of the Book of Mithira, Goddess of Magic."

I held up my hand, "Another time perhaps." I nodded to Dazz, who looked ready to fall asleep right there, and said, "Why don't you get a room for Dazz and we will continue our conversation in the morning. We have a lot to do tomorrow so rest up." They both made their way to the door and I nodded to them, "Good night gentlemen."

"Good night, your Grace."

Chapter 6

"Enter," I said in response to the knock at my door.

Sergeant Jur entered with Anton. I reached a stopping place on the list I was writing and placed the quill into its accompanying ink well, then asked, "What can I do for you gentlemen?"

They both bowed low. Anton, after straightening, said, "Your Grace, it seems that after you commandeered the Sergeant and his men, that the City Lord took it poorly. More than likely it was his wife, but the fact remains that they have been released from service."

Jur stood with arms folded behind his back staring at the wall behind me. Dressed in what I now knew as peasant's clothes of brown pants and an off-white laced at the neck shirt.

"And as they were in your service," Anton continued. "And under your protection, when they were let go; they were hoping for employment in your service."

I mulled that thought over a moment before grabbing a blank sheet of paper. After some terse questions about qualifications I started asking about family and ties of loyalty to this city and land.

I tapped my fingers on the table in thought. I looked at Anton, "They would need uniforms, yes?"

"Correct, my Lord."

"And equipment? Food? Do they know how to ride a horse?" The questions came to me rapid fire and Jur paled a little more at each one. "They will want to bring their families so more food and wagons," I said then pursed my lips. "Okay, here is what we will do," I looked at Sergeant Jur. "You and your men will swear to my family," he opened his mouth to reply, but I forestalled him with an up-raised hand.

"Your families can work for me, for a wage plus food and shelter, on the trip."

I looked to Anton, "We will put together a trade caravan for our trip through the Duchy."

He nodded and said "Very good, Milord."

"Get a mercenary company under contract for escort." I pointed to Sergeant Jur, "You and your men will be our personal guards."

They both bowed and I said, "Get our men equipped and seen to first Mr. Kos. Then the mercenaries."

Anton nodded, "As you wish, your Grace."

"See to it gentlemen, you have two days," I said.

The merchant I met before, Safira Pereira, joined us almost immediately. She traded in general household goods. Pots, pans, cutlery, and various other items that made a house a home. She also, for a small fee, delivered mail along whatever route she took.

Two other merchants joined us. Lord Martel Jahiem, a slight effeminate man, with a soft voice, who carried himself with quiet dignity. He, a landless third son who, with his mother's blessing, took his inheritance early to make his own way. Five years later and after a run in with bandits he was down to his last silver Marks. His work ethic and knowledge impressed me enough that, for a percentage of his business and repayment, I loaned him enough gold to purchase trade goods. He dealt normally in seed, and still did, but also branched out into farming equipment at my request.

The last merchant, not counting the guards family's, was a clothier who sold fabric wholesale. Dasra Shree, usually sold to tailors and seamstresses, but would also sell to villagers and homesteaders whenever he passed through. The side of one wagon dropped down and pulled out with a cutter to measure out then divide up whatever a customer needs, never "Letting a customer go to waste," as he would say. He also sold exotic spices from his home country of Binsar, like saffron, clove, cumin, and turmeric. He had a wagon full of spices, "Since these barbarians do not know how to season their food, at all!"

For the remaining families I gave out interest free loans so they could buy cheap knick knacks that I suggested they sell with an upcharge. This was just one of the benefits that I wanted to introduce for serving my family.

The real challenge in hiring mercenaries was finding a group that wasn't bandits themselves. Note to self: sponsor a guild or something that will self-regulate their members.

Captain Fallah's group wasn't recommended as being unreliable, but probably won't kill you in your sleep. It took an extra two days to find a solution. We contracted a separate pair of companies that didn't hate one another. The first, called The Order of the Sword, was a newly chartered cavalry company led by Lord Jasen Jellinek. Jah-sen, not Jason, is the second son of a landless noble who didn't inherit anything.

He joined the Kingdom army and worked his way up to Captain. After five years of chasing down thieves and riding border patrol, he sold his commission to a Baron's son, and created his company three weeks ago. Twenty-five men and fifty horses, all with their own equipment, would escort us to the city of Montenegro.

The second company, also Twenty-five strong, I chartered

myself. They would be based out of Montenegro and the start of The Free Company Mercenaries Guild. All had a minimum of one year of close quarters combat experience. Ten were marksmen with the short bow while the rest specialized in the short sword and shield. All of them wore leather armor. When we got to my city these men would be the trainers and administrators of the Guild. Pay for five years would start after our safe arrival, so they were motivated to do their best.

Anton did excellent work organizing everything, making sure everyone had a place to sleep, and delegating assignments where needed. Bed rolls to cook pots, cooks and foodstuffs, and feed and water wagons for the horses; he made sure we left with everything we would need.

I signed any paperwork he put in front of me. I even read some of them. Not because I didn't trust him, it doesn't make much sense to give minimal instruction for a task and not trust them, but because I wanted to stay abreast of the progress.

Most of the time, Dazz and I, learned magic. His natural talent is healing, using his own energy. My pamphlet of three healing spells left Dazz drained. So as part of his curriculum he worked on expanding his capacity to hold mana.

I made sure to continue working on my own projects. Inspiration struck after I made a breakthrough on my light spell. My problem was with trying to visualize something intangible. A triangle, square, or Goddess forbid a parallelogram, with a few symbols inside, wasn't all that difficult. But, the more complex configurations, for a shield or homing bolt of force, increased the orders of magnitude of difficulty.

By shaping my conjured light into the clockwork gears of the necessary shapes that rotated counter to the symbols inside, I made progress. I began to layer them three and four deep, trying to get the effect I wanted. The explosions of light when I failed, shocked the guards. At first. They were soon inured from the flares and flashing as my failures piled up.

Anton knocked on the door frame after the latest burst of light. The edges of the papers on my table fluttered. A little. But, it was a tremendous improvement when light could move an inanimate object!

"Your Grace, all preparations are complete," he bowed. "We can move at your earliest convenience."

"Excellent work Mr. Kos," I said. "We will leave after breakfast tomorrow."

"Of course, your Grace," he bowed again and left.

I had a carriage. A grand carriage, gaudy and pretentious, and blindingly white in the morning sun.

"It was the only thing available on short notice, your Grace," Anton said as he wrung his hands.

"I said I didn't care, didn't I?" I asked despondently, my shoulders sagging. "Maybe the dust of the road will cut down on the shine?"

Anton coughed gently, "One of the enchantments repels all dust, dirt, and mud from all surfaces on and inside the carriage." He sounded as if reading from a brochure. "Ensuring that, my Lord, will always be at his best?" Yup, sounds like a sales pitch. Anton's voice got smaller as my frown grew, until his spiel ended up a question.

"Does this," I paused for emphasis. 'Monstrosity', have temperature control?"

"Yes, your Grace!" Anton jumped on any positive note like a life raft. "It even has a new innovation! A box that will chill bottles and keep foodstuffs preserved."

"That is impressive," I said while trying to look suitably impressed. He nodded vigorously enough for me to fear for his health.

"The Queen is the only other person who owns one, your Grace."

"Then I am glad that I have you to help me keep the trappings of my position Mr. Kos." I clapped him on the shoulder. "Let's get started, my friend." I frowned in thought.

"My Lord?" Anton asked.

"I have another wagon I'd like to retrieve. But, it is in a difficult to reach spot, and even harder to get back to the road."

"We won't let you down, Milord."

I nodded to him, "Excellent. Please detail five men for the retrieval and I'll draw up a map."

"Very good, Milord," Anton said with a bow then walked off with celerity.

The carriage, for all its glittering pretentiousness and luxurious comfort, didn't have springs; but, it wasn't as bad as I expected. It had cushions of magic. One could still have a drink without spilling it everywhere. And Dazz and I could still practice our magic in peace. Minor things, but every little bit helps.

The merchants stayed to their wagons and didn't socialize with the other families. Viewing them as competition. They were rowdy in the evenings at first, the excitement of a new start spilling over. The days and weeks of slow travel, ground that exuberance away, with monotony and hard work.

The mercenaries did their jobs escorting us during the day, and guarding us at night. Lord Jasen Jellinek kept his troop professionally distant, keeping his men disciplined and sharp.

I'd promoted Sergeant Jur to Captain and gave him command of my company. His training regimen was grueling. Turned out he used to be one of this world's special forces soldier. A down on his luck elite trooper working as a guardsmen for a provincial backwater like Olasa. If there is a goddess of luck, then she really smiled down on me.

For the first few weeks I slept in the carriage. As comfortable as it was to ride in, it didn't sleep very well. I could hardly contain myself when my wagon rolled into camp almost a month later.

"Mr. Kos," I waved to the fire he shared with Dazz, beckoning him to me.

He bowed to me after he rushed up. "Your Grace, how may I serve?"

I winced internally. Sometimes the wording got to me. I was okay with someone working for me, as an employee. But, the overly salacious manner, like my shit didn't stink, made my skin crawl. Maybe I'd get used to it, though I doubted it. I justified the behavior as cultural differences, and tried my best to treat Anton, and everyone else, with respect. Most times it made the obsequious behavior worse.

"I'd like for my wagon to be cleaned and readied, please," I requested. A week into the trip, I attempted to clean and make a place to sleep in the carriage. You might have thought I'd done horrible and unspeakable things to his puppy. The man was a nervous wreck for three days afterwards. After I confronted him, Anton admitted that he thought that I repudiated his work, and that of anyone else in the camp. I acquiesced to the watery unshed tears in his eyes when he asked me to leave these tasks to him and his staff. I didn't know he had a staff.

"Very good, Milord. I will see to it personally." It seemed he was determined to make up for whatever perceived slight he'd thought up, to excuse my weird behavior.

The wagon's condition was as I'd remembered it, and so after a month of travel, I got a good night's sleep.

Two months of travel was surprisingly uneventful. Anton's advice for a heavy escort through a countryside devoid of people seemed a waste. The Duchy of Neves and Montenegro, claimed vast tracts of land; though they didn't have either the people, or the infrastructure, to utilize the natural resources abundant in the region.

Three days from the village of Boardlin, a pair of Captain Jur's scouts galloped up to him and gave a whispered report. I was too far away to hear, but by his body language, and the way his head jerked, to look at the route his scouts used to return by, the news didn't sit well with him.

"Dazz, Mister Kos, close up the carriage," I ordered. Dazz looked at me with his face scrunched up, but Anton moved with alacrity, punching a panel with a closed fist. The interior darkened as metal plates slammed closed. A soft blue light lit the inside while muffled shouts could be heard outside.

I took a deep breath, calmed my mind, and began spinning up patterns I'd started practicing a few days ago. I hoped it would work. White circles enveloped my arms and fists. Each ring moved independently of the others, containing its own individual glyphs, placed in the air before me in a larger overlapping spell form. Sweat beaded my forehead as my mind strained to keep everything precisely in its place. The spell snapped into place and a small jagged window tore open in the space between me and the world outside the carriage, showing me Captain Jur. I could hear him ordering his men into a defense formation.

When he paused I barked a command, "Report Captain!"

"Sir! Goblins," I started and the portal flinched along with me. "Sighted, headed this way. Thirty, maybe as much as fifty. Raiding party, well armed," he paused to take a breath. "Lord Jellinek is taking his cavalry to flank them while we turtle up here to draw them in here, Milord."

"Excellent Captain! Carry on," I let the struggling tear in space snap shut and fell back in my seat. Sweat plastered my hair and made my beard itch.

"My Lord," Anton started, I held up a finger stopping him. I breathed deeply. The spell almost got away from me in my shock, and I didn't know what would have happened. Maybe nothing, though I doubted anything good could come of it.

Fatigued, but my mind cleared again, I looked at Anton, "Goblins, Mister Kos?"

He looked at me confused for a moment then nodded.

"Yeah, we don't have them where I come from. What are they capable of and what do they look like?" I asked.

"Yes, your Grace," Anton sat primly with his hands folded in his lap. "They are odious little creatures. They have the intelligence of young children, but are vicious. They are primarily carnivorous, though can, and will eat anything; even offal and feces." Anton visibly shuddered. "They are thin and spindly, and don't get much taller than four feet. They are more commonly three feet in height." Anton, pale with a sheen of sweat on his forehead, looked like he would be sick. Dazz, sitting beside him, patted Anton's knee, but jerked his hand back at the sharp look Anton gave him.

With a deep breath Anton collected himself. "My Lord, they are cruel, torturing their victims for fun. Often eating them alive. Individually they are weak. On par with most children. But, their numbers can seem endless. Often wearing down those they prey upon." A single tear traced down his cheek and hung from his quivering chin. "A whole Malignity of the beasts will swarm through a village. Killing and eating everything before them," Anton said, staring sightlessly through the carriage wall. "Even through the cellar door, I could hear my mother's screams. There was nothing I could do." His manic eyes pleaded with me. "There was nothing I could do! We were poor and there was only space for one in the hole! She shoved me in! There," his voice broke, and he choked back a sob. "There was nothing I could do," he whispered in anguish, hugging himself. Dazz gathered Anton into his arms. He stared at me with steely determination above Anton's head. I nodded to him.

"Anton, my friend, you must not blame yourself," I grasped his shoulder firmly. "Your mother was a heroically brave woman. She saved you, her son, in the only way she could." I patted his shoulder and sat back. I didn't know exactly what to do or say and it made everything I tried seem hollow. "We should all be so lucky to have someone who loves us that much."

Anton's muffled sobs almost drowned out the muted shouts outside the carriage.

Chapter 7

Tap. Tap tap. Taptaptap. Anton, composed after a couple of hours, released the metal plates sealing us in. Dazz reached over, squeezed Anton's hand, and quickly made his way out of the carriage. Anton jolted upright and looked at me wide-eyed. I smiled and nodded to the door.

Exiting the close stuffy carriage into the waning light, I

breathed deeply of the evening air. And nearly gagged at the charnel house smell. I resisted the urge to wave my hand in front of my face. It wouldn't do any good for one, and I'm sure it would lower the opinion of the men, mercenaries and merchants alike, of me. The pampered noble made squeamish of the smell of the bodies they tossed into a bonfire.

Captain Jur came to attention and saluted me, fist over heart, and said, "Your Grace, we have eliminated the threat with few casualties. A handful of men have some injuries that we are treating now."

I looked over at Dazz, "Drazan, if you would?"

He nodded and quickly stepped to a tent on the far side of the wagon fortification.

"Thank you, your Grace," Jur said quietly.

"No, thank you. You and your men. Your bravery, quick thinking, and discipline saved the people here. You and Lord Jellinek are to be commended," I reached out to shake Jur's hand and after a moment's hesitation, he grasped mine firmly.

"Of course, Milord," he said simply with gratitude clear on his face. His eyes glanced over my left shoulder and I turned. Lord Jellinek strode toward us with a smile.

"Lord Jellinek," I said loudly. "Your flanking maneuver was

brilliantly timed." I strode the last few feet between us, reaching my hand out for his. With the way politics and courtesy worked in this world I couldn't bow to him. And just a handshake could be seen as scandalous, but I couldn't do anything less for someone who risked their life for the people in my care.

Jellinek's eyes widened briefly; he flashed a bright smile, and shook my hand firmly. "Your Grace, I'm honored." He released my hand and bowed low.

"Please," I said. "Pass on my thanks to your troopers."

He rose and said, "Of course, your Grace. They will be thrilled that you thought of them."

I turned slightly to face Jur, "We will want to move further down the road before we make camp for the night."

"Why would we, your Grace?" Jellinek asked, his expression puzzled.

"Because," I said motioning to the blood soaked ground. "If we stay here we risk disease. And I'm sure the scavenging and carrion animals will show up to this grisly feast."

"I don't understand, Milord," Jur said. "Disease is caused by bad spirits, and while a battlefield can have them, I don't see how you could know if they were around."

I tried to think of a way to explain germs to someone who'd never heard of them before.

"Captain, you have 'good' spirits in your gut," I said. Jur shook his head violently.

"No, Milord. I mean no disrespect, but every soldier knows gut wounds go bad quickly. They are almost always fatal."

"Captain, let me explain please," I waited for him to sheepishly nod before continuing.

"Your gut has 'good' spirits," I held up a finger as I saw his face turn obstinate. "But, they don't like the air. Exposing them to the air makes them turn 'bad'."

Both Captains' jaws opened in wonder. It was difficult not to shake my head. I made eye contact with both of them.

"Your 'spirits' don't like anyone else though. And if the spirits leave your gut with your excrement, they will pass on to someone else as 'bad' spirits," I gave them both a meaningful look. "That's why I had you dig the latrine away from camp."

"Oh," Jur said. "I thought you just didn't like the smell." He had the grace to look chagrined.

"I'm not fond of the smell, if I'm being honest. But, I don't want people getting sick, especially when it's easily avoided," I looked at both men sternly. "All latrines will be dug well away from water sources."

They didn't look totally convinced, though they nodded along. Fine.

"Am I understood?"

"Yes, Milord!"

"This will be done. Every. Single. Time."

"Yes, Milord!"

I smiled at them, "Excellent! After we've made camp, everyone will wash up, yes?"

"Of course, Milord!"

"Very good, gentlemen. Please continue with your duties. I will have Mister Kos organize the caravan to move on for a few more miles."

They both saluted smartly and rushed off. I looked around, saw Anton directing a pair of older women carrying linens and headed over to him.

The women scurried off as I approached and Anton turned to face me. "Milord, how may I serve?"

"Mister Kos, I would like the caravan to camp for the night at least a few miles down the road," I gestured to a particularly offensive piece of offal. "Will you make sure everyone is organized properly for me?"

"Of course, your Grace, it will be my pleasure," he kicked a goblin head towards the fire. "If you will excuse me, Milord?" I nodded and he left, stepping gingerly around pools of blood.

Dinner for everyone that night consisted of jerky, flat bread, and dried fruit around small fires.

I looked over to Anton across the fire sitting next to Dazz and said, "Mister Kos, please remind me that we need to pick up more food stuffs and maybe a chef at the next populated stop." I smiled to make sure my words didn't sting.

"Of course, your Grace."

Which is why I stared suspiciously at the sky several days later after Anton, Dazz, the Captains, and I came to the only Inn in the village of Boardlin.

"We don't need no extra spices in the stew!" A plump matronly woman shouted after shoving a rotund dark skinned man out the door. "People like the stew just how it is!"

The man, who couldn't have been much over five feet, whirled on the woman, and shoved a sausage thick finger under her nose. "Madame, I was leaving of my own accord." He shook his finger, "Do not touch me again!"

She took a step back, reached around behind the doorway, and slung a heavy pack at the man's head.

He fell back with a grunt as his padded rump hit the hard packed dirt.

"There! I didn't touch you none at all!" She went back inside, slamming the door behind her.

I reached up and pinched the bridge of my nose. I'd be willing to wager that this man was a chef, or at the very least a cook.

"Mister Kos, if you would, please secure rooms for our party. I would like to sleep in a bed tonight."

"Of course, your Grace, right away."

"Your Grace?" A voice questioned softly from under a pack in the dirt.

"Captain Jur, if you would be so kind as to help the gentleman up?"

"Yes, your Grace," and he lept upon the struggling man, snatching up the pack with one hand, and slowly lifted the man by the scruff with the other.

Jur released the man as the stranger gained his feet, but held on to the pack. I looked at the man expectantly.

He coughed and gave a florid bow. "Your Grace, please allow

me to introduce myself: Sin-Nasir, Master chef of the Kingdom of Akkad, personal culinary artist of the late Lord of Apai, head assistant to the Grandmaster chef of Queen Bila Ashenafi, second assistant in charge of," he stopped when I raised my hand. I realized he would keep going, probably going all the way back into his infancy if I let him. He was well spoken with a smooth baritone voice so I was almost tempted, but I wanted a real bed more.

"Very impressive, Master Sin-Nasir," I nodded to him. "I am Duke Montenegro."

He bowed low, although less excessively, "I am honored, your Grace."

"Tell me, is this," I gestured to the village around us. "Where do you wish to settle and make your home? With all of your accomplishments?"

"No, your Grace," he bowed so low he nearly folded in half. Which, considering his large belly, was outstanding. "I seek a patron to delight, one who can challenge my skills, and help me find the inspiration to create my grand masterpiece."

"I must say, I am quite impressed with your eloquence," I nodded as if coming to a sudden decision.

"Would you be willing to undertake a test of your skills?"

"Of course, your Grace. It is expected and welcomed to one

seeking patronage."

Anton exited the Inn with a frown.

"Excellent,' I said then turned to Anton. "Mister Kos, please give Master Sin-Nasir three Crowns." I turned my full attention to Sin-Nasir. "Tell me, Master Sin-Nasir, what would be more challenging, a test under ideal conditions, or one under poor circumstances?"

"Poor circumstances, your Grace, undoubtedly," he said with a frown.

"And for you personally, Master Sin-Nasir, would you be willing to undergo such a challenge of your skills and talents?"

Sin-Nasir's eyes widened as Anton pulled three gold Crowns out of his purse. "What are the conditions of the challenge, your Grace?" He asked confidently.

"You will be given three Crowns to purchase whatever you need to create a meal for six, under camp conditions. I also want to see a meal plan for the next three months, with the inclusion of at least two celebratory feasts, under road travel conditions. Will you accept my challenge, Master chef?"

Sin-Nasir's grin stretched across his face. His even white teeth are a stark contrast to his handsome dark features. "Yes, your Grace. I accept your challenge, gratefully." He bowed low again.

"Very good, dinner for six tomorrow evening." I turned to Anton. "Mister Kos, if you would see that Master Sin-Nasir has access to the encampment?"

"Of course, your Grace," Anton said, then looked to Captain Jur.

Jur nodded and raised his fist into the air. Five figures separated from the shadows around us. Jur pointed to one of the dark haired men and said, "Radlovic, see to Master Sin-Nasir's needs."

"Sir!" Radlovic saluted fist to chest then motioned to the chef to follow him.

I turned to Anton as the two men disappeared in the dark, "Is all well, Mister Kos?"

Anton sighed, "As well as can be expected, Milord." His pinched and sour face belied his words. "The Inn only has three rooms available. Drazan and I will sleep in the common room, so the Captain and Lord Jellinek will have the rooms across and beside your own, your Grace."

I frowned and Anton hurriedly explained, "They will be there to guard your honor and person, your Grace."

"Very well." I nodded, I thought somewhat graciously to him. "I will defer to your knowledge of the customs," I said.

We entered the common area of the Inn. The expansive room contained six long tables with a pair of long benches each. A large hearth held a big black cauldron hung from a cast-iron swing anchored to the floor. A pleasingly plump woman swiveled the contraption out from the low fire in the fireplace, ladled two bowls full of a thick brown stew, pushed the pot back with her foot, and carried the food to customers across the room.

"What can I get you for, my Lords?" The older woman who gave Sin-Nasir the boot asked.

I looked to Anton because he had expressed, at great length, to me that single eligible bachelors did not speak casually to members of the opposite sex.

"Madame Ingrid, my Lords will take a table with your evening fare, including two loaves of bread and beer for all," Anton said stiffly.

"We're happy to serve you, Lords. If'n you'll follow me?" She strode off as though marching to battle.

Anton muttered something that sounded like, "savages," under his breath. I smiled at the woman's simple ways. She reminded me of a southern Belle I'd once dated. As long as she didn't say, "Bless your heart," we'd be fine. Probably.

The meal, like the Inn and village surrounding it, was simple.

These weren't my people, though they were probably very similar to the people of my Duchy. At least those on the outskirts of cities and along the borders. People struggling to survive, working from sunup to sun down, didn't cultivate the same customs as those who had more free time on their hands. The safety to seek their fortunes is what I wanted to establish for my people. This settlement could very well have been a smoking ruin if the goblins got here first.

Chapter 8

The bed wasn't something a modern person would like, but after sleeping on straw filled cots, it felt good. A good night's sleep helped me tremendously. I still waited for the other side of Lady Luck's coin to show itself.

Drazan and I spent the day in my room practicing our magic and reviewing my books. I needed to make a decision soon about the direction I wanted to take my power; internal or external source. I could keep my Core small, but draw mana continuously from my surroundings. Or I could grow my Core to hold more at one time, and slowly draw in mana. Both philosophies had their pros and cons.

Channeling meant less energy from my body, and while the mana in my sphere of influence would regenerate on its own, I could use it up and keep the saturation point low. Another consideration is that the potential for a large burst of power is much lower from channeling.

Forming a Core on the other hand is a slow and arduous process. Creating a nucleus, then compressing it into a kernel, growing multiple kernels to then compressing them into a fledgling core. One is still not done, and the process is even more difficult as mana must be gathered around the Core and squeezed into the shell from one's channels. Which calls for strengthening the channels that have their own difficulties. This is not a method that is often used by practitioners, so finding guidance would increase the difficulty of my task.

The maximum capacity one could hold is exponentially greater with a fledgling Core, when compared to channeling, in a mana rich environment. Greater bursts of power is a plus, as well as the ability to continue using magic, in an environment depleted of mana. Such as when multiple Wizards, together, all channel mana in the same area. Which is precisely, one of the many dangers I anticipate, when facing my nobles. I could only depend on myself for defense, against other Wizards. I needed a Core.

Drazan though, because of his talent and affinity, couldn't form a Core. He could, however, widen and strengthen his channels. We would practice those exercises every morning, as I needed to do them as well.

After a lunch of bread and cheese, most people only ate two meals a day. I focused on learning how to meditate. Meditation is a needed skill when creating a nucleus and later kernels. Absolute attention is imperative. Deviations of the beginning foundations will create imbalances in the channel connections. Which in turn will hamper mana regeneration and power flow rates. Problems become multiplicative further along one's progression. So, do it right the first time.

Lord Jellinek, Captain Jur, and myself met Anton and Drazan by my wagon for dinner that evening. Foldable tray stands stood by chairs already laid out for the five of us, with a sixth place that would remain empty. I wanted to see his reaction with things not going to plan. Though judging by his round figure, he wouldn't have a problem with extra food being available.

Sin-Nasir, along with a boy of about ten—who looked just like him—carried out trays holding heavy clay bowls filled with a fragrant liquid.

"My Lords," Sin-Nasir said. "We will be starting with golden mushroom soup."

They served me first and the other diners waited for me to take the first bite. An explosion of flavors hit my tongue. The musky mushrooms mixed with some onion and garlic flavors.

"Master Sin-Nasir," I took another spoonful into my mouth. "What wine is this that I'm tasting? It is wonderful."

Sin-Nasir beamed. "A port wine that was locally available." His smile disappeared, "A true shame, your Grace. A Marsala would truly make the dish shine."

I nodded along knowingly. I hated having to substitute ingredients in my own dishes. To be fair, I was never a chef; I just enjoyed cooking.

We all devoured the soup with gusto. Anton, the very soul of propriety, shocked me by picking up his bowl and drinking it down. Drazan looked just as shocked as I did. But, we all soon followed his example.

Sin-Nasir and the boy quickly gathered our dishes and passed out small lemon cookies that were light and crisp, leaving our palates refreshed.

"Next my Lords, we have braised pork chops along with smashed potatoes and seared broccoli."

The dishes were handed out as before and I took the first bite as custom demanded. The pork was juicy and tender. I'd never had potatoes done this way before. It wasn't off-putting, a boiled salt potato that was then smashed. Delicious. The broccoli was blanched then seared in the same pan that cooked the chops, picking up some of the flavors and seasoning.

"Master Sin-Nasir," I said after wiping my mouth. "That was amazing. Thank you."

Sin-Nasir smiled and bowed low. The boy with him did as well.

"I would offer you patronage," I said as he stood upright. "But, I'm not entirely sure what that entails. Would you educate me, sir?"

Sin-Nasir seemed taken aback for a moment though he recovered quickly. I had the suspicion that he'd be one hell of an ambassador. "Your Grace, patronage, from your side," he paused for a moment. "It would be to provide funding and opportunity for the one, under your benevolence, to flourish."

I nodded and said, "I see. Thank you, Master Sin-Nasir. One more question if you will," I paused for his acknowledgement and he bowed again. "What does the beneficiary of such benevolence do in exchange for these considerations?"

"Ah, therein lies the crux of the matter, your Grace," Sin-Nasir said. "I would, of course, see to all of your culinary needs. There are times in which your Grace might need more esoteric activities completed. Knowing the foods that are fit for consumption also means I know those which are not."

"I see, thank you Master Sin-Nasir," I nodded to him in respect. "I would be honored to be your Patron."

"My Lord is too kind. I humbly accept, your Grace, and will put forth my utmost effort in any endeavor in your service," Sin-Nasir bowed low and held the pose for several long moments.

"Mister Kos," I looked over at Anton to see I had his attention. "Please see that Master Sin-Nasir has everything he needs."

"Of course, your Grace," Anton said, then approached Sin-Nasir, who handed over the list and schedule to Anton.

"How much longer do you wish to stay in Boardlin, my Lord?" Anton asked me.

"One more day, Mister Kos," I said. "That should give everyone a well deserved rest and enough time for the merchants to do business." I took out several one-hundred Crown notes and passed them to Sin-Nasir.

"Master Sin-Nasir, we have a spice merchant who has some interesting varieties that you might be interested in."

"Outstanding, Milord," Sin-Nasir enthused.

My people were busy the next day making trades, purchasing supplies, and performing any maintenance of equipment or vehicles as necessary. I, on the other hand, did not have any tasks as such. Anton complained enough that I just gave him a list of personal items I wanted in lieu of collecting them myself.

Bored sitting in a room alone, I informed Drazan to see that I was not to be disturbed, and began the lengthy process of forming my core. My channels did not exist the same way my blood vessels did, nor would my Core. Everything about Mana manipulation was metaphysical and depended heavily on imagination. The books explained that I needed a space to collect the mana I gathered to begin the compression process.

As this would be my foundational layer that all my progress depended upon, I needed to think and plan out the geometry needed. A basic education in physics I hoped gave me an advantage in this. Mana seemed to act as a low pressure gas so I needed a mechanism to convert it into a high pressure liquid.

Then increase the pressure again to crystallize the mana into an energy dense Core. A condenser coil came to mind first, but would take increasingly complex imagery to implement. I didn't want to depend too much on the mechanical forces of mana density in whatever environment I might be in to determine my progression. I needed enough mana to power through any opposition when we got to my capital.

So not a coil in the traditional sense. Not that any of this was traditional in any way that I knew of. What if I made a spherical chamber that connected my five input channels that attached to my main Core? Each aperture inlet would have a one-way valve. One like Nikola Tesla invented, that didn't use any moving parts, the valvular conduit. It wouldn't prevent total loss during down times, but it would allow for constant compression while I slept or any other time when not cultivating.

So, one chamber that I'll call the heart, that I can compress during cultivation. That in turn pumps into my Core. Both the Heart and the Core will need a backflow preventer in the multi-teardrop design which would increase pressure in the entire system.

The Heart would be a hexagonal sphere that honeycombed down to the valve. Because "Hexagon's are the Bestagon's," according to CPG Grey, if I remember his YouTube video correctly. Gotta give credit where credit is due. Anyway, the tops of the hexagonal tubes would be wider than the bottoms so when I mentally squeezed the structure it would compress the mana to a higher pressure liquid that would flow into another layer of tubes that are shorter to another layer, and so on. From there it would flow into the valvular conduit into the second chamber, the Core, increasing in pressure to begin the crystallization process. I hoped.

I closed my eyes and began visualizing the main space for these chambers. This would be the spot my Core would fill eventually. I made it large. To the point of being insanely optimistic, because why not? I conceptualized it behind my heart and above my lungs. In this void my Heart chamber and Core were placed. If I could connect them to my organs the process would be automatic. But, none of these things actually existed. There wasn't a physical mechanism to a Core. Mental energy manipulated mana where I wanted it to go. I needed this mental structure as simple as possible so I could keep it in my mind for as long as possible. Moving parts would increase the stress on my mind to the point where it just wasn't feasible to cultivate in this manner.

After the chambers I slowly built up the one-way valvular conduit. The flowing teardrop shapes alternated in a straight line beautifully simple in design. Once the entire mental apparatus settled into place, I began connecting in my five main channels.

At first, everything worked as it should. I let mana begin collecting in the Heart and the "weight" at the tops pressed the mana into the smaller chambered layers. It worked similarly to atmospheric pressure.

Then it stalled out. There wasn't enough pressure to force the mana to the lower layers and into the valve. I mentally squeezed the Heart, and forced the mana into the lower layers, but when I released it, the condensed mana would vaporize and escape. I needed a way to increase pressure without making hundreds of check valves.

The idea I came up with was coiling tubes that decreased in diameter, from my channels to the Heart. Spiraling channels that wouldn't let mana back through as easily. It wasn't perfect, but it worked for what I needed for now. I would have to invent another system to force my Kernels into a proper Core.

Twilight darkened my room when I opened my eyes. It took hours and hours, but my mental construct held. I was proud of myself. Through all these new customs and culture I didn't have too many chances to do things for myself. Being part of the leisure class didn't help either. So having an accomplishment of my own gave me a little pep in my step. It felt good. Dinner, as I would come to expect, was fantastic.

Potato soup, honey glazed duck, rice, and carrots. The spices were interesting, and complimentary, to the food and each other.

I checked my Core before bed and found that the mana started to form a hazy mist. It felt good, falling asleep with a smile.

Chapter 9

The mana mist in my Core wasn't any bigger than before I slept. But, the ambient density in the room was much lower, which made sense as I constantly pulled the mana into myself faster than it could replenish. Satisfied, I dressed quickly, and exited the Inn. I wanted to get on the road so I could begin the long process of cultivation.

Anton made sure the camp broke up quickly and efficiently and we were on our way. I'll be honest here. I don't want to boringly describe a long montage of training on a boring journey. Travel by horse is faster than walking. Though, not by much, when you are used to traveling seventy miles an hour. Twenty miles a day by wagon is a great day. A great day!

We didn't see other people for three weeks after Boardlin. And that was at a homestead family of five. We expected to reach the city of Montenegro in another four to six months. Another month before we entered the Duchy proper then a further three and a half weeks to the next town.

We, and by we, I mean the other people of this caravan, hunted for supplemental food choices, gathered water and herbs, and enjoyed the scenic vistas. I cultivated. That's it. That was all I did. My method helped me advance much faster than my books led me to believe. I went through mist and nebula within two weeks, and formed a Kernel in the first month. That was where I ran into my first of many problems.

Once a Kernel is formed, mana won't stick to it in a liquid or gaseous state. So I needed to move the Kernel before I could form another. I figured out how to suspend it in my space. What should actually be my Core. So now I have a Heart, a Bladder, and a Core. Now I have to figure out how everything from this point on works as none of my books contain the information. I did learn that two or more Kernels want to, not only stick together, but to rotate around the central part of my Core. My hope is that an increase in mass will compress the Kernels until it grows into a proper Core.

Another problem, if we stayed in one place for more than a day, was that I depleted most of the ambient mana in the area. For the most part it was fine, but I worried for the future of my cultivation, and my new home.

I couldn't use the mana I cultivated for spells. It all went to forming my Kernels. As such, my ability to communicate with those around me dropped precipitously. Sin-Nasir took it in stride, poor Anton though, thought I was mad at him for something or other. That Kernel took three days to form before I could take a break, and comprehend the language again.

I explained to him that I used a spell to communicate and he promised to get me books to help with the language. I didn't hold much hope from there. I remembered my horrific semester of French in high school. I didn't hold out hope for success.

During that stop, I also learned that I stymied Drazan's craft, because I monopolized the mana in an area larger than expected. Our caravan took up a total area of about one acre. I, slightly, exceed that amount.

So, between his need to see to the health of the people and animals of the caravan, and Anton's proclivities, I set a schedule for my cultivation. Three days to gather and meditate, and one day to take care of any business that might come up.

The mercenary companies got along well for the most part. The shared danger of the goblin raid birthed a high level of comradery, and rivalry. There has, from what I've heard, always been a contention between cavalry and, well, anyone not honored enough to be cavalry. The infantry, who held the goblins off long enough for the cavalry to come prancing around to flank the disorganized mob, did not take the ribald comments about sheep kindly.

Some practical jokes may, or may not, have been taken too far. My Captains knew their jobs, so I let them do it. Why they came to me for some things I didn't know, but I just asked them what they thought should happen, told them to do that, and they left happy.

I didn't think that the merchants should have any problems with each other. That couldn't be farther from the truth. Each sold different items, each camped separately, and they all accused one another of stealing customers from them. I asked Sin-Nasir to see about the truth of the matter. He said it was natural and that they were trying to keep competitive between settlements. Just another headache.

Thus, a week from the town of Betin, we used the local bandits to ease our frustrations.

"What do you have for me, gentlemen?" I asked as Captain Jur and Lord Jellinek walked up to my campfire.

"Your Grace," both men saluted in lieu of bowing. They began that practice after coming to me for advice about their men. "Our scouts have discovered a small encampment of what look like bandits about a week ahead of the caravan."

"Why are the scouts so far out ahead?"

"Milord, the scouts can travel much faster than this crawling pig of a caravan," Lord Jellinek said, and to his credit, tried to keep the sneer off his face. He and his men chafed at the slow pace of the wagons.

I scowled at him and he ducked his head, the tips of his ears turning red. "Thank you, Lord Jellinek," I said briskly. "Captain Jur, ideas?"

"Your Grace, his lordship and I," Jur gestured with his thumb to both of them. "Plan to draw the bandits on horseback into a line of infantry then sweep them up with cavalry."

I nodded for him to continue when he paused.

"Then the cavalry will swing around and push the stragglers to us to mop up."

"Will we take prisoners?" I asked. I couldn't think of a way to hold them if they surrendered, but I didn't want to let them go back to prey on other travelers.

Both men looked at me like I'd grown another head. "Your Grace, the penalty for banditry, is death,"

Jellinek said. "They won't surrender. Even if they do, it is our duty to see justice done."

I nodded slowly.

"Milord," Jur said carefully. "I understand that these settlements are claimed on maps, but the truth is, they have no one to help them in times of need," he shook his head sadly. "If we don't see to justice, many other innocent people will die."

"Your Grace, the Captain speaks truly," Lord Jellinek said, his face serious. "If we allowed a few survivors to flee, then they would seek out easier targets to prey upon. Often smaller, more isolated, families," he clenched his fists by his side. "They would allow no survivors to tell the tale. Even children."

"Very well, gentlemen," I said. "Do what must be done."

Both companies left the caravan that day. Leaving behind a squad of cavalry and infantry each so as not to leave us totally unprotected.

"Mister Kos," I said when we stopped for the night. "Have everyone circle the wagons tonight."

"My Lord?" Anton asked. "I don't understand. What circle?"

I frowned. It could have been that Anton didn't know because he didn't normally travel, but it seemed strange to me. "Please have the wagoner's come see me before they unhitch the horses."

"Of course, your Grace," I saw Anton mouth 'circle' as he hurried away.

The wagoner's didn't know the term either. I squatted down and drew a number of boxes lined end-to-end in the dirt. "We want to make a wagon fort," I looked around the gathered men and women. "The last wagon should have the smallest team to leave a smaller gap in the circle."

A large burley woman with a square jaw frowned, her unibrow scrunched, asked, "Milord, what's for? Can't see no reason to be working harder."

Several of the teamsters visibly winced, but it was an honest question after a physically demanding day.

I nodded and asked, "With most of our guards away, wouldn't you like to make it easier for those who remain to protect you?"

"Don't know that I'm the one needs protecting," sweat beaded on the brown hair of her lip. Then she added, "Milord."

I could see she was uncomfortable speaking with me. "I see. What about the children?"

"The young'uns?" Her face reddened. "Well sir, we'd want to see'm safe like."

I nodded, "Exactly. We want to see them and everyone else, safe. So we circle the wagons to make a fort. We block off most approaches and narrow down where an enemy can get to us from."

She nodded along with me, her short brown hair barely moved with the motion.

"From there we can place guards inside to patrol around to make sure no one sneaks in under a wagon. All the animals will be corralled inside with us so they can't be stolen either."

The others nodded along now. Nobody wanted one of their

horses to come up missing.

"So a little more work now means we'll be safer tonight," I said.

"What about in the morning, Milord?" A stout dark haired man with a cleft lip asked.

"Last in, first out," I said, scratching my beard. It took a moment, I could see the moment when the realization dawned for him. It happened sooner for others, but soon everyone understood. Even if there were some whispers that I purposely ignored.

"Mister Kos," I said over my shoulder. "Please help these gentlefolk," the teamsters laughed. "Work with our other companions to see this done adroitly."

Anton nodded and said, "Of course." And louder, "Your Grace."

The teamsters all shrank back and said, "Your Grace."

I turned so they couldn't see me and smiled at Anton's smirk, then leaned in and whispered, "Play nice."

"Very well, your Grace," Anton grumbled.

I walked away to find our remaining guards to talk about watch schedules. The mercenaries looked skeptical when I explained what the teamsters were doing. One cavalryman even scoffed openly.

"Milord is playing soldier now?"

Now, I didn't expect everyone to bow and scrape for me. Hell, it made me uncomfortable, but I had to put up with it. I didn't mind coarse language, bad manners, or uncouth behavior. What I wouldn't stand for is blatant disrespect. The other mercenaries looked on in astonishment.

"What are you lads looking at?" He gestured to me. "You've all heard how soft he is," he smirked. The men all looked at me.

I cleared my throat roughly. "Gentlemen," I made eye contact with each man. "What is the disciplinary action for insubordination?"

The cavalryman took a step back, "Your Grace, that won't be necessary." He held out his hands pleadingly, "I won't ever do it again, Milord!"

The other cavalrymen grabbed him first. I watched two of the infantrymen run off.

"Rope and whip, Milord," a stout infantryman explained. I nodded.

"Your name, cavalryman?" I asked.

"Ustin," he sputtered. "Yanovich, your Grace." He stopped struggling and hung his head. "Sergeant First Class Ustin Yanovich, sir." He dangled listless between the cavalrymen.

The two infantrymen ran up and stopped, huffing, "Sir! Rope and whip, Milord."

"Cavalrymen," I asked. "Who among you will bear the burden of dispensing punishment to Yanovich?"

"Your Grace," A slender man with a serious face said. "Lieutenant Sergei Boydalo. I will dispense punishment, if it pleases you," Boydalo said then bowed low.

I nodded, "When you are ready Lieutenant." If I issued a punishment, then I would witness it as well.

Otherwise, I had no business handing it out.

They tied an unresisting Ustin Yanovich to the side of a wagon, stripped to the waist baring his back, his arms secured above so his toes scrabbled in the dirt.

"Sergeant Ustin Yanovich, you are accused of willful misconduct, insubordination, and contempt of a Noble, witnessed by those present," Lieutenant Boydalo stated, his posture stiff and unyielding. "What say you?"

"I, I apologize, your Grace," his voice muffled by the wooden side of the wagon. "The fault is entirely mine and the punishment just."

The Lieutenant looked at me and I nodded to him. "Because of your acceptance of your faults, your lashes are reduced to ten, from thirty. May Týr grant you mercy."

Boydalo unfurled the whip and muttered, "Because I will not."

Yanovich grunted at the first and second lash. He cried out by the fourth. His screams were hoarse by the eighth when he passed out.

Lieutenant Boydalo gestured to the infantrymen and they let Yanovich down gently. Drazan took a hesitant step forward. I didn't notice when he joined me in my vigil.

"Lieutenant," Boydalo looked at me sharply. "When can the Sergeant be healed?" I asked gently.

He let out a pent-up breath, "In the morning, your Grace. He has to survive until sunrise."

I nodded, "He's a strong man, he'll make it."

Sergei Boydalo took a shuddering breath and nodded to me. "Thank you, your Grace."

"Of course," I said. I grabbed Drazan and led him away. Then I saw the crowd that had gathered. Merchants, teamsters, mothers, and children all looked at me with varying expressions. From anger to openly weeping. Some even nodded.

"I will say this one time," I faced the crowd, voice raised to be heard. "I will forgive malapropos due to ignorance or earnest enthusiasm." I met every eye I could, as I looked over the people assembled before me. "But, do not treat my kindness for weakness. I will not brook outright disrespect to me, my officers, or my staff." I held my head high while I let my words sink in, then I walked away. My stomach gurgled queasily and I felt like an imposter.

Ustin Yanovich survived the night. Drazan healed him just as the sun touched the sky. If just barely. I didn't mention it, and neither did he. We didn't get attacked last night. Nothing and no one came up missing. Some of the teamsters grumbled, quietly, about the unnecessary extra work, but better safe than sorry.

The rest of the mercenaries met back up with us just before the evening meal. Lord Jellinek almost ran through my campfire to bow before me.

"Your Grace," his pallid and sweaty face gave weight to his ardent plea. "Please forgive me, my Lord. I am a reflection of my men and their dishonor is mine." He collapsed to his knees, face in the dirt.

I could feel the eyes of the people upon me. "Lord Jellinek," I said loudly. "All dishonor has been washed away in blood. The punishment dispensed, and the crime forgotten. Please, arise anew, and with your honor intact." I wasn't sure just how far he'd go, I didn't want to risk his life when it came to honor.

Not if some simple words could prevent an unnecessary sacrifice.

"You honor me, your Grace," Jellinek stumbled as he got back to his feet. Surprisingly, Anton was there to catch the man and kept him from falling on me. A flash of metal in the fire light, there and gone, before I understood what happened.

Anton patted Jellinek's back and nodded in reply to the lordlings' thanks.

"Was it really necessary to have the poor man flogged?" Drazan asked.

Captain Jur answered before I could, "Absolutely," Jur folded his arms across his chest. "The chain of command is sacrosanct. Men live and die on the word of their Commander. Anything that undermines that authority puts every soldier at risk."

"But, he could have died," Drazan argued.

"Were it up to me, he would have," Jur scowled. "I'd have executed him myself."

"But, why?" Drazan asked incredulously.

Jur glanced at me. It was quick, but he'd been caught and he knew it. Jur pointed at me, "Because Duke Montenegro is different. He gives respect without demand. He takes advice. It's almost like he's human."

I raised an eyebrow to that last one. He shrugged. I shrugged. Impasse.

"And a man deserved to die because our Lord is human?"

"No," I said.

"Yes," Jur said emphatically right on top of me. He bowed to me. "Your Grace, rare is the chance a man has to serve with honor."

I bowed to him. Jur, at the show of deference, wilted and squirmed uncomfortably. I smiled at his distress, "You flatter me, sir."

"Your Grace," Jur trailed off. He seemed at a loss for words.

Chapter 10

Betin came into view as we crested a hill. One of many we've traversed. It got to the point I could almost predict the pattern of them. Which I thought odd enough to take note of the geological feature. I was positive that an aerial view would reveal concentric rings like in a tree. The crater resulting from such an impact would be enormous.

The wooden palisade of Betin looked much the same as the one surrounding Boardlin. Well weathered sharp tipped logs bound together with tarred rope. Occasionally a head would pop up looking out at us as we made our slow way to the gates. The gateway was just large enough to accommodate our caravan single-file. Most of our group would camp out outside the walls on the other side of the town proper. The mercenaries would rotate leave schedules for some time off.

I looked to Anton, beside me in the carriage, "We will leave in three days. That should be plenty for the merchants, and the soldiers can enjoy Betin's hospitality." Knowing just what they would enjoy. "I will not hold up the caravan because someone did something to end up in jail."

Our carriage was the first to enter the town. A knock on the door had Anton opening it up to a slim man in a blue and gray uniform. He didn't wear armor like the other guards of the town, though his helmet had a crest of black feathers.

His gray eyes took us all in and the sneer on his lips said he wasn't impressed. "Do you men have any magic-users traveling with you?"

Everyone in the carriage looked at me. And that drew the attention of the slim crested man. "You?" He scoffed. He shook his head. "You are hereby under arrest, all your personal effects are to be confiscated, and the trial will be scheduled for some time when I can be bothered."

Lord Jellinek and Captain Jur flanked the official on either side and Jellinek asked, "Is there a problem, your Grace?"

Slim went pale and wobbled on his feet.

"Lord Jellinek," Anton said. "It appears that Duke Montenegro is not welcome to the town of Betin. They are attempting to arrest, and if I'm not mistaken, extortion of my Lord's person."

"Your Grace," Captain Jur began. "Should we burn the town down now, or wait until after looting this pigsty?"

I looked down at the official who'd collapsed into a puddle of what I suspected of his own urine.

"I will not stay in this town," I looked at my Captains. "I know how much the men looked forward to a break though so I would not take this opportunity from them."

Jur pointed at Drazan and Dazz hung his head. I smirked.

"The merchants need to do their business quickly though, and," I looked at Anton. "Sin-Nasir will need to restock as best he can. We leave in two days. Tell our driver to turn the carriage around if you will."

"At once your Grace!" Jur saluted.

In the end only Sin-Nasir entered the town despite numerous messages sent my way with flowery sniveling and groveling. The mercenaries unanimously decided not to give their hard earned coin to the town. The merchants came to an accord based more on politics than any respect they had for me. They figured that the loss of future income would be greater than the minor loss of this small town. In all honesty, I didn't care one way or the other about what the merchants did. They were a convenient excuse to travel with as many troops as we did.

After another delectable meal prepared by Sin-Nasir, Anton approached my fire with a short man, who almost ran to keep up.

Anton bowed low and grunted as the newcomer didn't immediately match his posture. The stranger wore his paunch poorly. His overly large head, skinny upper body, and bulbous abdomen gave him a weird pear shape that reminded me of a heavy drinker that quit too late. Red spider veins seemed to crawl across his greasy face.

"Your Grace," Anton said as he rose to his full height. "The Mayor of Betin has graciously donated a large portion of his personal wealth to the church of Mithira and the local orphanage. All for the pleasure and purpose of apologizing to you." He gestured to the Mayor. "Mayor Sinclair, your two minutes have started now."

I frowned at the sleazy Mayor as he dry washed his hands and bobbed his head. He seemed at a loss for a few moments.

"Your Grace," his voice wasn't as disgusting as the rest of him. It was smooth and soothing. Something made me want to listen and I found myself leaning forward. "Please forgive my man for his rudeness before you had the chance to see our beautiful town."

Well, it wasn't like I was in any danger in the town. Forgiveness was supposed to be a good thing anyway.

I nodded my head, and Mayor Sinclair smiled knowingly.

"Furthermore, your Grace," Sinclair's cringing manner fell away and he seemed to force the sneer from his lips. "And while it is quite regrettable, you will need to turn yourself in to the constable. As the practice of magic is prohibited in and around the town's environs." He nodded and I followed suit. "All of your material possessions will, of course, need to be confiscated to be inspected for magical taint. We have a clean town and want to keep it that way."

It seemed reasonable. I wasn't above the law. Or was I. That was a confusing thought and I frowned.

Mayor Sinclair paled and sweated profusely. His sudden odor of rancid alcohol nearly bowled me over. I took a step back and shook my head, my thoughts cloudy.

Everything snapped into focus and Sinclair snarled, "This is why Wizards aren't allowed into Betin!"

He lunged forward, a dagger in his fist flashed in the firelight. I stepped back and to the side. Sinclair tripped over my camp chair. I knelt and touched a large splinter of firewood, teleporting it into the Mayor's head.

Mayor Sinclair shuddered, his feet tapping out a macabre tattoo in the dirt, then quickly fell still.

Anton shuddered and fell over. He retched, the acrid smell of his vomit wafted along the gentle night breeze. He coughed and hacked out a filthy wad of something or other, then spat to clear his mouth of the no doubt vile taste, trying in vain to regain his composure.

My little camp was in tatters. Broken chair and table pieces littered the immediate area. I heard several shouts in the background, but I couldn't see far beyond the immediate firelight. There. My wine skin lay in the dirt by the fallen Mayor's corpse. I bent over and picked it up.

I looked over to Anton to see him sitting back on his haunches and called out to him, "Anton." He looked up at me.

"Here," and I tossed the skin to him.

He croaked out something unintelligible. I nodded and waved to him.

Captain Jur ran up to me, saw the body, and began shouting into the darkness, "Form up on the Duke! Protective ring, now!"

Jur adjusted the position of his men while I saw to Anton. "Are you okay, my friend?"

"Your Grace," Anton sniffed and ran the back of his hand across his nose. "I'm so sorry. I don't know what happened." He wiped at his eyes. "One of the guards informed me of an important message so I went to investigate myself. The messenger appeared quite distraught and earnest so I… I'm not sure after that, your Grace." Anton shook his head sadly, a despondent look on his face.

"My friend," I said. "Don't worry about it. You had no defense against his magic."

Anton broke down and wept.

My throat tightened and fists clenched. I wanted to burn Betin to the ground! I wanted to rage out of control. But, attacking the town is tantamount to declaring war on a rival Duchy, for one. And the people of the town didn't know what happened. They were innocently living their lives. Well, maybe not innocent, just ignorant of this shit stain's actions.

In the end, I didn't order the sacking of Betin. Foodstuffs and the like were purchased. A few hours after sunrise, the town dropped out of sight, behind the ring of hills. It wasn't a satisfying decision, though the thought of killing that many people, even by proxy, disgusted me.

I didn't cultivate today. Instead I focused on learning my shield spell. The concept part came easily, though holding the different spatial shapes and runes, made my head feel like it split open. Using my illumination trick flooded the carriage with bright light, which also made it more difficult to concentrate.

"My Lord," Dazz pointed to a passage in the Arcane workbook. "It says here if you relax your concentration with the light, 'the intensity of the illumination, will lower to mirror the strength of one's intention.'"

Dazz frowned. "Does that make sense?"

"Yes Dazz, it makes sense," I shook my head. "It means I've been a try-hard."

"My Lord?"

I waved off his question. "I'm excessive in my exuberance."

I chuckled at myself. Next thing I know, I'll be aggressively ambivalent.

"As you wish, your Grace."

I canceled my light spell and the spell formation of the shield. It took several embarrassing tries to get the level of illumination I wanted. The light blue glow of Arcane energy traced out the paths of the symbols that I thought necessary for a shield. As I worked through them I realized that I was trying to represent a three dimensional protection with a two dimensional script. With a mental push, I shifted the circular spell forms into a sphere. The symbols shifted suddenly into place with a psychic click.

A curved dome flashed into being before me. The blue glow lasted only a moment before the whole thing faded away. Reaching out, my hand stopped at the solid shield in front of me. I traced it down to the floor, then up to the ceiling of the carriage. It worked! I couldn't keep the giddy grin from stretching across my face. I looked at my fellow passengers to share my excitement with them, to find them both asleep.

Anton, with his head on Drazan's shoulder and their hands clasped together, looked peaceful. He deserved a reverie after the wizard attacked him with psychic energy, or more commonly called, Mind magic.

From the little I know of it, mana naturally helps protect against its use, psychic energy is limited in its application against another wizard or magic-user. But, the vast majority of people have no defense against this power, like Anton and the mercenaries. They were victims, plain and simple, defenseless to the power of a Mind Defiler.

Lord Jellinek spoke about it afterwards.

"I could have been worse," Jellinek shook his head sadly. "I've seen the aftermath of the filth these pieces of shit Inflict on others." He looked at me soberly, "Anton and the others, they don't remember. Probably because he wanted to get away with whatever he had in mind. But, it could have been much, much worse."

My spirits soured, I dismissed the shield. A horrible thought occurred to me. I pictured myself flattened between the magical barrier and the back wall of the carriage as the vehicle was torn apart. I mentally reviewed the spell, checking to see if I included it to move with me. I sighed in relief. I had. This wasn't something I should leave to chance, in the future.

I spent the rest of the day building a spell that was a staple of all wizards: an Arcane Projectile. Call it a bolt, a bullet, or a missile; it still served the function of hitting a target at range with the intent to damage or kill. I wanted an unerring device to carry the energy to the target; I soon realized that the complexity of the spell form remained out of my reach. I could, however, fire a pulse of energy from the palm of my hand rapidly in a straight line. I couldn't very well test it in the carriage, but the symbols looked promising.

Sin-Nasir's dinner that night: grilled trout with honey lemon drizzle and wild greens. I was lucky to find him in that village. I kept my cheeks clenched waiting for the price the goddess of fortune demanded.

Chapter 11

We crossed the invisible border into my domain on a rainy day. The rich soil turned to black mud, slowing our progress. Most merchants came to Montenegro via ship, so the roads into the Duchy were in poor repair.

The first true town, a week after we crossed the border, was called Risin. Dark gray stone walls, fifteen feet high, surrounded the town. The north gate spanned two wagon widths. Made from oak and banded with iron, the sturdy gate stood tall and proud. Scars marred the surface, and scorched markings told a story of hard use. They were also closed to us.

"What do you mean you can't let us in?" Captain Jur shouted.

"Goblins sighted, Milord," a voice replied from the top of the wall. "Be best if you found shelter quickly."

"No shit, you horse's ass!" Jur's face turned an ugly shade of purple. "That's why we're here!"

Lord Jellinek rode up beside my carriage and shook his head. I nodded to him then called out to Jur, "Captain Jur."

He looked back at me sheepishly. "Yes, your Grace?"

"We are in no immediate danger."

"Yes, your Grace," Jur turned his attention back to the wall. "Get your Commander over here. Please."

"You have a Duke with you?" A helmeted head slowly peeked over the edge of the wall.

"Yes, lad," Jur sounded resigned. "Just get your commanding officer over here to meet his Grace."

"Which one?" The voice asked.

"What?!" Jur's blood pressure flushed his face red. "The highest ranked officer you report to!"

"No, no. Which Duke is here?" The man's voice grew more confident.

"Your Duke, you twit!" Spit flew as Jur shouted.

"We don't have a Duke," the man paused a beat. "Everybody knows that."

"You do now!" The purple color returned to Jur's face. "Why do you think a Duke would visit your podunk little town out in the middle of nowhere!"

"Then why's he here then?" The wall guard asked incredulously

Jur turned to me and asked, loudly, "Permission to storm the gate, your Grace?"

"Hey now, there's no call for all that," the guard complained.

I smirked at Captain Jur. He scowled at me, realized what he was doing, then bowed low.

I raised my hand, exposing the mark, when I got closer.

"What's that now?" The guard asked.

A sudden clang sounded and the guard stumbled forward, catching himself on the top of the wall, only just stopping before he fell over.

"Your Grace," a loud gruff voice called down. "If it pleases you, the gate will open in a moment."

Just as I was about to reply I heard a muffled, "Yes now, you moron. I swear, if you weren't my sister's friend's nephew I'd throw your arse over the wall to the goblins." A pause. "No, I just don't want to listen to your mother's shrill voice complaining for a week."

The gate opened smoothly and just enough for the wagons to enter one at a time.

"If they try to arrest me," I said to Jur. "Or have made magic a crime." I made sure to look my Captain in the eyes. "I want the heads of the leaders of this town."

Jur saluted, fist banging his breastplate, "As you command, your Grace."

Lord Jellinek and his men formed up around my carriage while the infantrymen followed close behind. I directed the driver to park off to the side, so as not to block the rest of the caravan. The last out of the carriage, I took the opportunity to look around while Anton decided who spoke to me first.

Risin was clean. Shit didn't stain the stone walls of the buildings from where people might empty chamber pots from windows. Refuse didn't litter the alleyways that I could see. And most importantly, it didn't stink of human and animal waste.

Anton and a pale man with dark hair stopped before me and bowed. "Your Grace," Anton said. "This is the Captain of the guard for Risin, Reed Samson."

"Your Grace, on behalf of Risin," Reed bowed low again. "Please allow me to apologize for the rude reception you received."

I nodded, "No harm done Captain." I gestured laconically to the buildings around us. "I am quite impressed with the cleanliness of your town, and I would like to know how you keep it so, but," I waved to the gate. "You have a problem with goblins?"

"Thank you, your Grace. Of course, your Grace," Reed began to visibly sweat. "Occasionally, your Grace."

I nodded amicably, "Is there a Mayor, or Lord, to whom I might be introduced?"

"Of course, your Grace," he snapped a crisp salute, did an about-face, and marched away. "If you will follow me, your Grace."

I raised an eyebrow at Anton, which sent him scurrying after the nervous Captain.

"Lord Jellinek," I said to get his attention. "Would you be so kind as to meet the town leadership with me?"

"I would love to, your Grace."

"Captain Jur," I continued when I had his attention. "Would you investigate the goblin problem? If we can eliminate the problem before we travel, I'd be grateful."

"I will see to it at once, your Grace," Jur saluted me then began ordering five of his men to escort me and Jellinek.

My guard detail formed up around me as we made our way down the street. My initial thought about the town folks' well-being was that they appeared happy. Which jarred against my speculation about how they kept the town clean: slaves. Which if true, I'd be responsible for a great many deaths. I held a position of power, and therefore carried a moral responsibility, to correct injustice. It wouldn't be easy, I wasn't naïve, I still wouldn't tolerate such an inhumane institution.

After a pleasant, ten minute walk, through the affluent part of town, we entered a well maintained estate. We walked through a decorative, white stone archway, and down a cobblestone walkway. A matching, white stone manor, high arching windows with dark trim, charmingly welcomed us. A majordomo waited by the dark stained double doors.

Anton bowed slightly to the man, "I present," he gestured eloquently to Jellinek. "Lord Jasen Jellinek."

He then, dramatically I thought, bowed low to me with a flourish, "His Grace, Duke of Montenegro, Lord Daniel Hawthorne del Montenegro."

The majordomo, who looked smug and slightly

condescending, paled at my introduction. He bowed so quickly he stumbled and would have fallen if Anton didn't catch him. Now Anton looked smug. He looked back at me and I arched an eyebrow his way. He winced and coughed lightly. I pretended not to notice him help the man.

The majordomo, cheeks flush, cleared his throat and louder than I thought needed, said, "My Lord and your Grace, please be welcomed to the house of Baron Nicholas Risin."

Both Jellinek and I nodded, then followed the majordomo into the manor. The entry was bright and airy. Several tapestries of landscapes hung from the walls. The majordomo was almost at the end of the hall before he stopped just before a door, knocked quickly, then entered. Anton kept our pace leisurely. I played along because I guessed it gave the majordomo time to get the Baron up to speed at our surprise visit.

The majordomo stood next to a slim older man. The crow's feet around the Baron's brown eyes and his salt and pepper hair gave him a distinguished look.

The Baron glanced at my markings and immediately took a knee. "My Prince, welcome."

My eyebrows tried to climb up across my scalp. I didn't know I was a Prince, but I didn't want all this…

Hell, I didn't know what to call it, kneeling to me wasn't

necessary.

"Thank you, Lord Risin. Please, rise," I gestured to his well stuffed chairs. "Can we sit? I have some questions."

"Of course, your Grace. What is mine is yours."

He waited for me to sit first before he did. The Baron clapped his hands and the majordomo darted into the hall. Lord Jellinek sat in a love-seat to my left. Moments later a flood of men entered the parlor with finger foods and a variety of drinks.

"Lord Risin," I nodded to him. "Thank you for your hospitality. "

"Of course, your Grace."

"I am most impressed by the cleanliness of your town," I said. "How do you do it?"

Lord Risin nodded proudly. "Ah, you noticed. Thank you. My wife said I needed something to keep me busy."

He gestured to the side. "So she came up with the beautification project. She gave me some resources and a goal and here we are." He smiled widely.

"It is excellently done my Lord," I nodded to him. "What method did you use?"

Eyes shining he said, "I set up a program to put the homeless to work. See, we had many refugees living on the streets. Families sleeping in the gutters." His voice grew passionate, "Children starved, crime rose, and filth stained the streets. So I developed a system to hire and house people who were willing to work," he clasped his hands together and beamed. "It's been a rousing success!"

I sighed internally as relief flooded me. The Baron was a likable fellow and I'd have regretted killing the man. "That is outstanding! Congratulations, Milord Baron," I said.

"Thank you, your Grace, you are too kind."

"Not at all," I said with a smile. We engaged in small talk for another half an hour discussing light things.

As we wound up the conversation I asked, "Is there a church of Mithira in Risin?"

The Baron nodded, "Yes, your Grace. I can send a runner ahead so that the Bishop can greet you, if you would like?"

"An excellent idea, thank you."

We left the manor house and followed the directions the Baron gave us. After about fifteen minutes we stood in front of a two story domed building. The sides and front that we could see were square, made from stacked white stone. Thin gray mortar made mystic patterns throughout the structure. The dome shined gold with white stone ribs arching bottom to top, supporting the structure. A black spire, trimmed in gold filigree, stood proudly. The gold starburst at the top of the spire, with irregular rays, crowned the church of Mithira.

A wizened old man in plain gray robes stood between two boys in white robes. The boy's brown hair had bowl shaped haircuts. Their light brown eyes were solemn.

The old man's wispy white hair, while smoothed down, seemed to reach out delicate fingers here and there that waved in the breeze. His blue eyes were cloudy, but alert and focused on me.

"Your Grace, welcome to the Risin Dome of Mithira," he said with a bow. "Please, call me Johan."

I returned his bow, "Thank you Johan. The Dome is wondrously magnificent."

"You are too kind, your Grace," Johan said with a smile. "Please, won't you come in? I would be honored to show you our humble arts to the glories of Mithira."

"Of course, Johan," I nodded to him. "Thank you."

We entered the church, brightly lit from thousands of candles. A dozen chandeliers hung around the circumference of the dome, many more multi-armed candelabras shown light on the tiled mosaics decorating the circular wall around the base of the dome. The ceiling of the dome itself was painted in a way reminiscent of Michelangelo's work on the Sistine Chapel. Instead of man meeting the Christian God, the Goddess Mithira, gave magic to humanity. It looked like a comet or something very similar to one falling to earth. Spell forms formed a halo around the goddess of magic and the plummeting rock.

On another part of the ceiling both the 'comet' and the goddess were absent and a firestorm washed over the land destroying everything in its path. The whole ceiling told the story of how Mithira gave the world magic and the recovery of the land. Blue portals dotted every panel. One with an empty hand passing through; another a booted foot, some with sandals, a few clothed, and some nude. There were several with baskets of different fruits and vegetables. People from different places. Different worlds?

Interestingly there were two groups who appeared in the backgrounds of some panels. Small green figures, who looked an awful lot like goblins, and larger green figures with tusks. An evolution perhaps?

We walked around the dome as Johan pointed out various holy objects and famous scenes of church history. In all honesty, I wasn't all that interested. In my past life, I was an atheist so religion here wasn't high on my list of priorities. The fact that I'd been marked by a deity blew my lack of belief out of the water. That didn't mean I'd suddenly turned into a zealot, or even worship the goddess, just because I had evidence I was lacking before. The goddess was only one of many ways to connect with the divine.

"Thank you, your Grace, for letting an old man prattle on," Johan said with a smile. "What can I do for you, your Grace?"

"Please, Johan, let's not stumble over formalities," I began, but Johan shook his head vehemently, to the point I feared for his safety.

"Your Grace, I could never."

"Fine, fine, to business shall we?" At his nod I said, "I would ask two things of you. One," I held up my finger. "Please have word sent ahead that I am on my way to Montenegro, and that I request that the Mithiraian church perform my official coronation." I added another finger, "Two, I want to partner with your church to set up centers of learning." Johan went pale at that. "I will, of course, provide substantial funds and tax exemptions for the operation of the school and admittance of a set number of students."

"But, of course, your Grace. One of the tenants of Mithira is of scholarship."

"That is good to hear," I smiled at him. "Because the institution should be non-profit. Thirty out of every one hundred students will be open to those less fortunate or unable to pay for their attendance. All fees and materials will come from a fund I will provide." I continued to smile while pretending to ignore the sweat that beaded on his forehead. "Courses will include, but not be limited to, natural science, arithmetic, reading and writing, magic theory, and magic practice and principles. Any questions?"

"I, umm, no?" The Bishop visibly deflated.

"Excellent!" I held my hand out to Anton and he placed a thick roll of scrolls in my hand. I handed them to Johan and repeated the motions again, only with a thick stack of banknotes this time.

"Thirty thousand Crowns should be plenty to build the school, hire staff and professors, supply food and materials to the students. For the next ten years. At least." I smiled again, "Don't you agree?"

Bishop Johan's knees wobbled as he held the notes and scrolls to his chest. "Yes, your Grace." Johan gulped to swallow the lump in his throat. "But, the Baroness, she can be quite, umm, harsh in her opinions of the lower classes."

"And if she were the one funding the school and scholarships, she would have a voice in how it is run," I waved a hand negligently. "If she becomes too much of a problem, then I will have her removed."

Johan hung his head and asked, "If you would follow me to my office, your Grace?"

I let Anton handle the particulars he and I previously discussed in the carriage on our long journey. There were many things I wanted to change and some to implement as new innovations. Most of them would not be popular amongst the nobility.

Chapter 12

While Anton finished, I sent one of our guards back to the Baron to set up dinner for tomorrow evening. After a few more pleasantries we made our goodbyes and left. Master Sin-Nasir, after dinner, complained. "Your Grace, with all due respect, the best the cook for the Baron can serve to you is swill. Suitable only for those who have lost all sense of taste. I beg you, please, allow me to use my humble skills to prepare something worthy of your personage."

I almost smiled at his flamboyant behavior, the serious set of his eyes stilled my expression. "Is this important to you?" I held up a hand to stop his immediate reply. "I mean truly important. This is not a whim, or a strong desire to practice your skills? Because, if I am to risk a slight to the Baroness, and make this a thing of politics." I lowered my hand, "It better be important to you."

Master Sin-Nasir bowed in half, "You do me great honor, your Grace." He rose, "More than you know."

Sin-Nasir then pressed his hands together, palm to palm, raised his right hand and kissed his fingers then touched them to his forehead and released the kiss to the sky above his head. "Your safety is more important than the questionable honor of your aristocracy."

"You suspect poison?"

"Probably not that far," Sin-Nasir tilted his hand back and forth. "More likely something that is off, to offend and leaving you feeling uncomfortable. But, even that has its risks." His expression turned solemn, "Your Grace, please allow your humble servant to use his skills to the utmost"

"Skills," my chin lifted as I looked at him. I tapped my lips with a finger. "I can see this going poorly for the Baroness."

I nodded decisively, "One of the courses will be something that can be prepared quickly. Your signal will be my spoon turned perpendicular to my fork. My knife will point to the target. Any questions?"

"None, your Grace," Sin-Nasir bowed. "Everything will be as you desire."

"Very good, Master Sin-Nasir. Then you have my blessing. See Anton about setting everything up and for an allowance to buy whatever you need."

"Thank you, your Grace," Sin-Nasir bowed again and almost seemed to skip out of the room.

The next day, I worked on my cultivation. In an effort to

accommodate my wishes, my dinner with the local nobility would be postponed until tomorrow. Anton was under the impression that the Baroness wanted to make sure that her daughter would be there.

"Why do you say that?" I asked.

Anton looked at me with an unreadable expression for a moment then cocked his head to the side.

"Your Grace," he let the statement linger for a long moment. "You are the single most desirable, eligible bachelor, in the Duchy, if not the whole Kingdom."

I groaned. "She has a daughter," I said.

"She has a daughter," Anton nodded as he replied. "And, I must say, probably thinks you are presenting yourself as a suitor."

"Wait. What? Why?" I felt the blood draining from my face.

Anton chuckled and ticked off points with his fingers. "You spoke with the Baron. You asked to have dinner with the family. You then made arrangements to have your personal chef prepare the meal. Ostensibly to show off and impress them. And lastly, they were not told a reason for your visit so they most likely made one up themselves," Anton shook his head. "Probably to prove how important they view themselves to be."

I hung my head, "I can't cancel now, can I?" I muttered.

"Not without giving greater offense than simply not pursuing the lady."

"Well shit," I said. "What do you know of the daughter?"

Anton looked up at the ceiling and thought for a moment. "Her name is Theresa Risin. She is thirty-six years old. Two children, a twin boy and girl, Edith and Nicholas II aged ten." Anton paused, scratched his nose, and continued, "I know her husband died in a goblin raid a few years ago, but I'm afraid I don't know the man's name. "

I shook my head to keep him from continuing.

"Does she not meet with your approval, your Grace?" Anton asked. "On paper it is a decent match, and she has proven her ability to bear children."

"That may well be, Mr. Kos," I said. "But, in this case it would muddle the line of succession. Who would inherit, those of my line, or her first born?"

Anton frowned in thought and I spoke again after a moment of silence, "Exactly my point. A war could be fought over this very point. At the very least, my children would have a higher risk of assassination from within the family." I shook my head, "It is not a risk I am willing to take, especially when all I have to do is be a little picky about whom I will marry."

"I see your point, your Grace. I can assure you that many others will not agree with your choice."

"Of that, I have no doubt, Mr. Kos. No doubt at all."

Now that we were in a moderately wealthy city, Sin-Nasir went all out on dinner that night. Dinner at the inn last night, a large bowl of stew and a loaf of dark bread, cost eight pennies; the smallest of the copper coins. Sin-Nasir spent twenty-two Crowns. Gold. On one dinner.

To put this in perspective, one hundred Pennies equal one Mark, and seventy-five Marks equal one Crown. The commoners mainly use copper, such as Pennies and Quarters, while merchants usually use silver coins named Marks and Lures. The nobles are known for gold Crowns and Royals.

Twenty-three different courses comprised of soups and salads, breads and pastries, fish, poultry, mutton, and beef. Vegetables galore and fruits out the wazoo, and the desserts. Master Sin-Nasir found chocolate. I wasn't sure where it existed in this world, to get more. Though I did have my suspicions on how so many of the new world foods from the Americas were found in these lands.

After the meal, I broached the intended subject of this meeting with the Baron. Which was a mistake, as the Baron wasn't in charge of anything, and that was my fault for imposing my own preconceived biases. Anton made it clear multiple times previously. The fault was my own.

"My lady, I truly meant no offense," I said for the fourth time. If I didn't need a bank in this location I'd have left already.

"So you've said," Baroness Meredith Risin said miserably. She portrayed the very picture of wounded nobility. "If that were true, you would agree to marry my sweet Theresa."

Theresa crossed her arms over her generous breasts and glared at me. Her soft brown hair and makeup were artfully done, and made her not ugly. But, she did me the favor of changing the subject, "If you didn't come to court me, then why are you here?"

I nodded graciously to her and faced her mother, "My lady, I wanted you to be the first to know about my opening of a branch office of the Bank of Montenegro."

"Duke Montenegro," Meredith's plain face scrunched in confusion. "The Duchy doesn't have a bank. No one has access to…" dawning compression blossomed over her face and her eyebrows rose to two bushy peaks.

"Yes, Baroness Risin, I do," I fought hard to keep the smugness out of my voice. I'm sure by Theresa's narrowed eyes I wasn't completely successful.

She pointed finger and shouted, "You never had any intention to court me did you?"

I saw Meredith cover her mouth with the back of her hand as I glanced back and forth between both ladies. I turned slightly to Anton beside me and asked sternly, "Did you or someone else on my staff mislead either of these ladies?"

Anton for his part replied with aplomb, "No, your Grace." He primly folded his hands in his lap. "I, as is proper, had no contact with either the Baroness, nor her daughter, Lady Theresa."

I nodded and muttered my thanks then turned my attention back to Theresa, "Lady Theresa, I apologize about any misunderstanding of my intentions. My goal, for tonight, is to lay the groundwork for the economic growth of the Duchy."

A sneer marred her face and she said, "What would a man know of economics? You should be busy trying to find a woman to manage your House!"

Theresa Risin slapped the table so hard the plates rattled and wine sloshed as glassware rocked.

"You impotent bastard! You have one job. One!" Spittle flew from her rage filled face. "And that is to produce an heir." She stabbed her finger at me accusingly, "A job you are failing miserably."

My knuckles popped as my fists clenched tightly. Anton rose

in his seat and placed a restraining hand on my shoulder. Captain Jur, previously ignored as decoration against the wall, reminded our hosts of his presence by the ring of drawn steel as he leveled his sword at Theresa across the table. The sword point didn't waver an inch under her chin. The same could not be said of her, as her knees wobbled and a tiny cut opened up on her shocked face.

Anton motioned to Jur, and the Captain lowered his blade. He did not sheath it though. Anton gave a single nod then faced the Baroness, "You will curtail your daughter, or you will need to find a new heir."

Meredith gasped, stood, and covered her face to muffle a sob.

Theresa's previously pale face began to flush as she smirked. A stinging smack sounded as the Baroness slapped her daughter full across the face. The red handprint stood out in stark contrast to the shock on her face.

"You will not speak to a guest in our house like that!" Meredith loomed over her daughter as Theresa plunked back down into her chair. "You dishonor yourself, and more importantly, this family with your behavior."

Meredith bowed low to Anton, much lower than custom and propriety allowed. "Please, forgive us."

My knuckles were still white as I glared at Theresa, who

wouldn't look at me. Anton waited three breaths before he said, "That remains to be seen. Rise, Baroness."

Meredith rose swiftly, and swayed, forcing her to grab the chair back in front of her. Her lips quivered.

"She doesn't know," Anton cut his eyes to Theresa. "Does she?"

Meredith shook her head mutely, but gestured to her daughter as Theresa opened her mouth. "You do not speak again."

Anton looked at the Baron and I followed his gaze to see Nicholas, pale and sweating, his eyes darted around the room. Anton turned his attention back to the Baroness.

"Blood."

A tear fell from the tip of the Baroness' nose.

"That is the price of dishonor. The Duke of Montenegro is not a country Lord. He is your liege, your suzerain, whatever you want to call it, and to dishonor him in such a way…" Anton shook his head. "The price is blood, if he so chooses. Not just the offender in this case. He was given guest rights by," Anton shoved his finger practically under Theresa's nose. "Your House."

Theresa flinched back terrified.

Anton nodded, "Exactly. Blood paid by the entire House."

Anton waved lazily in my direction. "His Grace is quiet now because," this should be interesting. I held my tongue because I wanted their cooperation with the bank. "If he speaks, this slight must be acknowledged, thus ending your House."

I stayed quiet. I didn't want to kill the whole family just because I got my feelings hurt.

"His Grace was here to propose a business opportunity for your family. One that would make you all quite rich. And," Anton bowed his head and paused briefly. "You get offended because he will not marry you?"

The scorn in his voice was palpable.

"You are a very small, minor House, on the Duke's own lands. He showed you an enormous amount of honor in your treatment, and you threw a hissy fit," Anton looked at each noble, making sure he had eye contact from them all. "It would take half an hour to eradicate your House, and raise a new one in its place."

The Baroness broke first. Her shoulders shook as she sobbed into her hands. The Baron closed his eyes and bowed his head. Lady Theresa, stared at her mother and father aghast, then promptly fainted. The thud of her body hitting the floor went unremarked.

I continued to let Anton have the lead, as he is doing much better than I'd performed initially. Anton waited for the Baroness to compose herself then continued.

"The town of Risin is the largest settlement closest to Neves, on a former trade route. With the infusion of capital a Bank branch provides, this town can become a major stop along the trade way," Anton began to pace, and continued his lecturing tone. "With guards sworn to the Duchy patrolling paved roads, we can compete with the intercoastal waterway in all but speed. Thus, we can keep the price of our goods down, the closer we get to the interior, and the far side of the Duchy."

Anton stopped and gave the Baroness his full attention. "All of this can be done without you, but," Anton held up a finger. "His Grace is willing to partner with you to oversee this area." Anton shook his head, "Before this travesty, you would have had quite a bit of autonomy, that is no longer the case." He looked at the nobles making sure he had their full attention. "Because of your daughter, you will forswear all other oaths," the Baroness gasped, again. "Yes, milady," Anton nodded. "And swear blood oath to his Grace. Your House will be irrevocably tied to him."

The blood drained from the Baroness' face as she looked to her husband. Anton waved his hand as to shoo whatever thought might have passed through her head.

"No Baroness, you may keep your marriage alliance, though your ultimate allegiance is to the House Montenegro."

Meredith breathed out a sigh of relief.

"Now," Anton produced a bound folder. "I have some documents that need your signature, my Lady, that have to do with the Church…"

Chapter 13

We continued our travels later the next day. Initially my thought was to hand over a bunch of bank notes to Lady Meredith, and there you go, a bank is made. Turns out it is slightly more complicated, and expensive, than that. My experience with banks was with fiat currencies, not physical commodities. The important distinction is that the bank in question needs to have the commodity itself on hand to back the promissory notes. Most of the taxes collected by Risin were in copper and silver so I opened an account and exchanged some of my gold for the smaller change metals. Only the gold changed hands, and a lot of paperwork was generated. It was all very complicated. I made Anton handle almost all of it.

The perks of an authoritarian regime.

The town of Star met my expectations of a medieval town. A nauseating mix of human and animal waste, garbage, and a tannery. The breeze from the nearby sea blasted the odor as we approached Star, so we all looked forward to leaving as soon as possible.

The town wall and buildings were made of a darker rock. It wasn't quite black and the eastern sunrise glimmered off the surfaces in town. Those not covered in shit anyhow. I decided that I didn't want to stay in an Inn here so I made Anton inform the merchants that, should they wish to stay, they would need to meet us outside the gates come sunrise.

Anton informed me that the local nobility wasn't in and that they would be terribly sorry that they missed me. It seemed they didn't like to stay here any more than I would. Dinner that night was stuffed Quail, greens, and what looked like purple potatoes.

Later the next day, we made it to the coastal road, and had one more stop in the town of Plav before we made the Capital of Montenegro. The city itself didn't have a name that anyone else knew, but everyone called it Montenegro.

I continued cultivating my mana while we traveled, very close to completing my core. Eight kernels made a loose sphere with space for one more. After that I would need to compress them down into a single metaphysical object. For the last several days the final kernel didn't want to slot in. The kernel itself acted like it had a will of its own. The books mentioned, briefly, a second path of specialization; it did not say it was a requirement though.

The normal Elements didn't resonate with me. The concepts were too simple. Necromancy was banned for good reason, and the taboo for mental control, that I didn't want, wasn't worth the risk of a peasant revolt for mere convenience.

My focus on Arcane energy gave me a great deal of flexibility. My powers encompassed Telekinesis, Light, and Space magic. The classical Air, Earth, Water, and Fire Elements were answers for the states of matter as the ancients knew them. Modern Earth science has progressed much faster than here. Pressure has just as much to do with the states of matter as temperature does. With space and telekinesis, I can change pressure, and mana to excite or slow atoms… Different ideas flashed through my mind. I could almost feel my neurons firing off as my body tingled through my epiphany.

The one lonesome kernel, changed color from the light blue of Arcane energy, to a deeper azure, then flashing to the red of a burning coal. Colors glimmered quickly, they didn't blur, each hue distinct and sharp; until the kernel flared into a white light, then faded to a vibrant indigo purple. An icy wind passed through me, then a raging inferno, I clutched my, metaphysical and metaphoric, butt cheeks, but the show was over. I gently coaxed the kernel into place. The chunk of ethereal mana clicked into place. It was the weirdest shit I've ever experienced. My core began to glitter and shine, a kaleidoscope of blues, red, indigo. I mentally braced for the joining. I wasn't ready. My core flashed white, then my consciousness fled, and I knew no more.

The sun still shone when I awoke with a start. The others in the carriage glanced at me, but went back to their own diversions quickly. I surreptitiously checked my body. Everything was as I'd left it. I closed my eyes and checked my Core. My intangible representation of gathered power was most definitely not how I'd left it. From my studies, and the information available to me, my expectation for how my Core should look, was that my second focus would occupy the corresponding amount of space that was put into it. If I dedicated a third, that is how much space would be filled.

My Core was indigo. All of it. And the density of power held a tangible weight in my mind. The Kernels were no more. In their place sat a glowing perfect sphere. It spun slowly on an axis that I felt in-line with my spine. I don't know how, or even why, I thought that. It just felt right.

I opened my eyes and grinned so much my face hurt. I was a Mage! I raised my hand before me and it lit with an indigo fire that didn't burn. I twirled my fingers about and the flames caused no discomfort or sensation.

"Mother of Mysteries!" Anton shouted. "Are you hurt?"

"No, my friend, I'm fine," my cheeks ached from my smile. "Better than fine, actually."

"Then why do you look like that, your Grace?"

I laughed. I probably did look a little crazed at the moment. I'm a Mage! And magic! This is a dream come true, and I couldn't wait to stretch these magic muscles out.

I scratched my beard as I thought about what magic I could try out in a moving carriage. Mindful of my previous realization that a stable shield could end in disaster.

So, I thought of the spell circle for my portal and it almost jumped into being before me. Previously, I'd struggled with the spell. Speaking with my Captains during a goblin attack took a lot out of me and used all my concentration to keep a small window open. Now, it seemed almost too easy. The open portal was about one foot square and looked down on our moving caravan. The spell circle allowed for two-way passage so I wanted it up and out of the way.

I took the opportunity that my long travel time afforded and thought about what different spells I wanted and needed. I thought about them in terms of the various games I'd played on Earth. My single target damage was unfair, and broken, to be honest. I felt confident that my teleportation spell could handle even a small group. A horde of goblins was another matter altogether. So, I needed some area denial/damage, an AOE spell.

I lost the ability to use internal magic with my spell focus and therefore couldn't cast any buffs. A similar problem with debuffs. My focus excluded curses, healing, and other internally focused magics. I could cast a bright flash of light to blind my enemies, but it would also include myself and any allies in the area of effect.

The intricate details of a spell circle formed after some thought. I'd gather the humidity in the air and then split the oxygen and hydrogen in the molecules, create a spark, and then watch as everything went boom. Yeah, I could work with that, though it would use a massive amount of mana to power the spell circle though.

The spell circle seemed to form an imprint to my Core as I memorized the spell. I made a variation of the iconic Arcane bolt spell. Indigo spheres of energy would orbit around me in a cloud as a defense. Or they could be sent out singly or in groups as an attack. I still couldn't get a homing function to work properly so they would fly in a straight line. The Arcane Swarm would use a moderate amount of my mana.

I learned a lot in my attempt to create a targeted cleaning spell, even though I couldn't make what I wanted. With my newly formed Core, intent did most of the heavy lifting in creating a spell circle, but I still needed the specific runes to form specific instructions. So, if I used it I'd be clean, of hair and clothing, and probably finger and toe nails. Maybe. I really don't want to test it out on myself.

Something that at first blush would seem wasteful, that I just had to have, was a way to cleanse the air around me. Say what you will about modern society, but sanitation technology, and basic hygiene, have made huge improvements in life expectancy and health. If most cities in this world smelled of the residents excrement, I expected that my own city would be no different. So, I created a spell to filter out noxious fumes and particulates. I made the pattern of acceptable air quality during a rest stop with a pleasant sea breeze. Anton thought I was crazy, again, for being so excited. He'd learn.

A constant mistake I made when I played RPGs was forgetting which spells and abilities I had, usually when I needed them. So, I'm listing them now:

Light ball

Telekinetic control

Molecular manipulation

Object teleportation

Arcane Bolt

Arcane Shield

Small Portal

Scorching Detonation

Arcane Swarm

Cleanse

Aura of Ambiance

Not a bad list of spells to have. If I knew the molecular composition of penicillin I could change this world. I don't. I took physics in college, but I majored in business administration. I know there are laws to thermodynamics, and at least three of them, all I could tell you though, is that order is not a natural state.

My Core pulsed, warming my inner being, and then settled down with a final flutter. So… I closed my eyes and inspected my Core. Still a vibrant indigo, the outer edge faded darker, to absolute black. It made a distinct border that I'd not noticed before.

"Anton!" I shouted. He started at my overly aggressive shriek. I mean, my assertive shout.

He held his chest while breathing heavily wide-eyed in terror.

"I'm sorry, Mr. Kos," I said. "My excitement is no excuse for poor manners."

"It's alright, your Grace. What can I do for you?"

"I need some writing materials. Pen, paper, notebooks, something to write with and on."

"Oh," Anton said, deflating a little bit. "I don't-"

"Here, your Grace," Dazz interrupted, reaching into a

backpack I hadn't noticed earlier. He handed me a fountain pen and a laced notebook.

"Excellent!" I said much too loud. "Sorry, thank you."

Dazz shook his head.

I opened the notebook and started to jot down my thoughts. My Core went through changes when I had either an epiphany, or an organized thought, specific to my focus. So, as a hypothesis the idea is workable. Now to test it out.

My focus is Arcane energy. As unaligned mana it is without elemental affinity so I gave it the label Arcane. It is a tale of what happens when not choosing a focus is a choice in and of itself. But, in this instance, it is just a form of energy, the name or title means little.

Matter bends space, matter and energy are synonymous, space and time are also synonymous. Though, does my teleportation break the light speed barrier? Time would move slower for the object in motion the faster it goes, so superluminal speeds could have a coin traveling to the past. Or maybe the coin's subjective past? That's getting a little too wibbly-wobbly for me. That could be why I don't hear a bam, or other sound of displacement. It was already there.

When I felt my Core pulse again, I realized that I really didn't want to teleport anymore. Would it be cool?

Undoubtedly.

Did the possible consequences outweigh the benefits? More than likely. But, I'll stick with weaponized teleportation.

I examined my Core one last time this cultivation session. In the area around my core, mana fell like spun wisps of cotton candy. It was a surreal experience. Did I just increase my mana regeneration by thinking about space?

Chapter 14

Plav was situated on the western side of the coastal road so while it had easy access to the sea, it didn't have direct traffic to and from. Knowing the people's propensity to throw trash anywhere, that was probably for the better.

The stone here, similar to my untrained eye, if not the same, as the type used in Star. The constant sea breeze kept any offensive odors down to a tolerable level. My new Aura of Ambiance negated whatever miasma was left over. What surprised me though, was the fact that as we got closer to the walls, my core filled with mana faster. To the point that I no longer felt the slight strain of my Aura spell. I jotted that fact into my notebook.

The gate guards were professional as we entered the city. And it was a city, at least to local standards. The level of technological advancement for the kingdom of Tallinn meant land was much more valuable for agriculture, since they didn't produce as much per acre, so the outright size of Plav made it a city.

The black, mana concentrated, stone was the main building material, and a few buildings contained three floors. The second floors were wider than the bottom so that most alley ways were covered. It made the main thoroughfares seem close and dim. Bright colorful sheets, pennants, and ribbons decorated the buildings and people. In all fairness, that one man might have been trying to hang a sheet and not wear it.

Reds, greens, and blues stood out cheerily against the dreary backdrop. The sea breeze snapped and popped different flags amongst the cacophony of human voices. The sheer volume of sensory input after the monotonous journey stunned me.

I didn't know where to look first. So, I settled on the people sharing the street with us. Their mode of dress was different from what I'd seen before. Robes were more popular here than in the other towns we'd passed through. They were loose and flowing, using bright colors, and could pass as a dress on some of the men.

Some of the women wore tightly fitted tunics of green with billowing red skirts. Others also wore garb that reminded me of Buddhist robes from movies, tailored to show off the attributes that the wearer presumably liked best. Some wore pants with the robes, others did not. Some were cut to show décolletage, while some were cut up the sides showing that many women and men, shave their nether regions. Which I found odd, as I'd been told that it was a fairly modern concept formed in America.

The social actions of sexes presented in a different way that took me a minute or so to realize. The men were more demure than I was used to. A woman put her hand on the small of a man's back as they crossed the street, another turned her head to get a better view when a guy bent over in front of her to pick something up off the ground, and several cat-called what seemed to be random passersby. The sexual dimorphism was the same as I'd been used to on earth and the other places I'd visited in Tallinn. So the cultural differences were jarring.

"Hey handsome," a dark haired woman in her thirties called out to me in a husky voice. I turned around, to make sure she was in fact talking to me, but no one was behind me.

"That's right boyo, I'm talking to you," she pushed herself away from the wall she'd been leaning against causing her unrestrained breasts to jiggle. She smirked when she caught me looking. "Like what you see?" She tugged at her robe to show even more cleavage. "I know I do," she licked her lips as she sauntered close, her hips moved with an exaggerated sway.

Her body shifted and moved in interesting ways under her green, gold, and orange robes. Nonplussed for a moment, shocked at the woman's brazen attitude, it didn't stop me from ogling her. Her smirk widened to a teeth showing grin.

"You can look all you want, boyo," she stopped and gave a twirl, the hem of her robe lifted a little and showed that she did in fact wear pants. She stopped with her hands on her hips and cocked an eyebrow at me. "Do you want dinner and a tumble, or just the tumble?" The tip of her tongue peaked out to caress the indentation of her cupid's arrow.

Anton coughed loudly behind me. I'd forgotten about him, and the others. The woman laughed saucily.

"Boys, boys, I like my men one at a time." Lord Jellinek barked a laugh. "Now, if you form an orderly line, we might could have some fun."

Anton gasped and poor Dazz's eyes looked ready to pop out of his head. Captain Jur grinned broadly and stepped behind Lord Jellinek. Jasen motioned for me to step in front of him. Anton regained his wit and growled out, "Your Grace should not perform depraved acts in public."

"My flat is just around the corner," the woman jumped in when Anton took a breath.

Anton ignored her and continued, "Nor should you fornicate with someone, not your wife."

"Mithira's muff, why ever not?" She turned to me angrily, "Have you been wasting my time? Are you so small you don't want the other's to see?"

"Are women that preoccupied with size?" I asked Anton.

"I wouldn't know, your Grace," Anton looked down as his face flushed.

I laughed and clapped him on the shoulder, "No worries, my friend, no worries."

The woman yelled out, "Help! I'm being accosted!"

Almost everyone on the street looked over and most continued on their way, as it was obvious that the woman was safe. Three men exited the street, and approached us.

"Oh thank you, kind and handsome, sirs! Please teach this man a lesson!" She squeezed the sides of her breasts with her arms and almost popped a tit out. The men ignored me for a moment until she gestured to them impatiently. They grabbed cudgels and advanced toward me.

I opened my purse strings and six silver Marks orbited around me. My Captains drew their swords and stepped in front of me. Five other men stepped from the gathering crowd, swords in hand, and advanced on the three bully boys.

The woman paled and pointed wordlessly behind the men she'd called to defend her honor. One turned and shouted, "We're surrounded, Mick!"

Mick looked at the woman, "Lady Minerva, what would you have us do?"

Her lip trembled, but she grit her teeth, and drew in a loud breath. "Please, Milord, don't hurt them, I'll do whatever you want."

I stared hard at her then smiled, "Excellent!" I said with faux brightness. "Go away."

The men looked at one another, and the people in the crowd murmured.

"What?" Lady Minerva asked.

"Go. Away," I said in the same fake happy voice people usually reserve for puppies.

Barks of laughter started up in the crowd gathered around us. Minerva walked stiffly away, but soon broke into a jog, then a run, as she fled the gales of mirth at her expense.

Captain Jur's men sheathed their swords and melted back into the crowd, on guard once again. Lord Jellinek put his weapon away as well, but Captain Jur kept his in hand as five men, in matching black, gold, and green robes approached our party.

One of the newcomers stepped ahead of the group and asked, "What is the meaning of all this?"

Anton stepped up beside me and said, "A slight misunderstanding is all..." He trailed off unaware of the name of the man.

"Sergeant Park. You can call me Sergeant Park," the man said brusquely. "What misunderstanding?"

"Where someone does not understand the intentions of another," Anton said, his jaw set and his back ramrod straight.

Sergeant Park pointed at me with his jaw, "He don't talk?"

"His Grace does, in fact, speak," Anton said archly. "And as his chaperone, he speaks through my voice. "So...?" Anton gestured to Park.

The Sergeant heaved a sigh, looking put upon, "Look Mr. Chaperone."

"Mr. Kos," Anton interjected.

"Mr. Chaperone Kos, did your man here," he waved a hand in my vague direction. "Set upon, and viciously attack, one, Lady

Minerva?"

"No."

Park scowled, "Are you saying that the honorable Lady Minerva lied?"

"Sure. Yes. Will that be all?"

"No, that will not be all," Sergeant Park looked to his men. "We'll have to take you into custody then to find out the truth."

"No, I don't think so," Anton gestured to me. "Are you then accusing the honorable Duke Montenegro of lying? Of stooping so low as to assault a woman who was already offering herself to a line of men?"

"That is preposterous!" The Sergeant shouted. "We haven't had a Duke in, generations?"

At his first shout, I began to remove my gloves. My marked hand was raised and presented before he finished. He stared, mouth open for a disturbingly long time.

"Sergeant Park? Are you okay?" Anton asked.

"But, but how?"

"By the Grace and Majesty of the goddess Mithira," you could hear the capital letters in Anton's voice. I wasn't sure how I felt about it though. On one hand I was essentially kidnapped, and on the other I was living my dreams. I wouldn't change it, I'm not a fool, but sometimes I felt off, like an imposter.

"But," Sergeant Park looked around in confusion. "The Lady said?"

I almost felt bad for the guy. He was in a tough spot, no bones about it, Minerva caused him this problem, though how he went about his business left a bad taste in my mouth.

I cleared my throat to get Anton's attention. He looked at me and I subtly nodded my head to the street.

Anton nodded and turned back to Park.

"Sergeant Park, his Grace has many things to do today. If you inform Lady Minerva about the status of the man she accused, you may find a different story than what was reported initially."

Sergeant Park nodded gratefully and ushered his men down the street with celerity.

"Well done Mr. Kos!" I clapped Anton on the shoulder. "I apologize for putting you in that situation to begin with. I'm old enough to know better than to engage with such a woman."

Anton sighed and shrugged his shoulders, "No need to apologize, your Grace. I fear you will have many more encounters and have to bear such things from the nobles in

Montenegro."

"Like with Baroness Risin," I asked him.

"To one degree or another, your Grace," We began walking down the street. "Wizardry often runs true through the female line, and there are more female magic-users than male. So the women are in charge of their Houses and lands," he ran a hand down his face. "They also choose their partners based on their own whims because they will always know who their children are from. There is no question of paternity with descent from the female line. They are always their children."

"I see," I nodded along. "It makes sense. Magic equalizes the dimorphism inherent in humans, so there is no need for a protective and supportive male force." I scratched my beard. "They will be quite shocked with me then."

"Quite right, your Grace," Anton smiled. "I dare say, it will be quite the scandal amongst the nobility. What with you having imposed qualifications for your future mate."

"Well, if I understand this mark correctly, then I will have proof of paternity no matter what," I shook my head. "But, where I come from, things are different, and I'm not sure I'd be happy with that lifestyle."

"A truly calamitous and outrageous flippancy of the natural order, since the unification of Tallinn, in the last three generations."

"Is that, sarcasm, I'm detecting from you Mr. Kos?" I pretended to be shocked.

"Never, your Grace," Anton said deadpan. "Such impertinence would never pass these lips."

I grinned at him, "Very well, Mr. Kos. I will, of course, continue to rely upon your help and guidance."

My words moved Anton to bow to me in the street, annoying some, and caused others to stare.

"Always, your Grace, always."

I squeezed his shoulder and said, "Thank you, my friend." I looked around, "Where are we going by the way?"

"There is a tailor just around the corner here, that I heard about in Risin, that is known amongst the nobility, as the best in the whole of Montenegro."

"Shopping, Mr. Kos?"

"Shopping, your Grace."

I hate shopping.

Chapter 15

The tailor's shop was a two story nondescript building on the main thoroughfare done in the same unrelieved black stone as the rest of Plav. The inside was almost as garish as the proprietor. Sheets of colored fabric hung along the walls, from the ceiling, folded up in cubbies, and stacked in rolls all around the open floor of the room. A man in a layered skirt of orange, yellow, and green sat working at a table towards the back of the room. He looked up as a bell jingled when we entered.

"Be with you in a moment," the man said.

We waited about five minutes for the tailor to finish what he was working on. "How can I help you?" He asked in an unsurprisingly high pitched voice as he stood up from his chair.

He was taller than my own six feet, though not by much, and very thin. Almost to the point of being skeletal. He moved with grace and confidence.

Anton stepped forward, "Mr. Silva, his Grace is in need of a wardrobe of the highest quality, and you come highly recommended."

Silva waved a hand at him, "Flattery will get you everywhere. Please, tell me more."

What followed was a flowery and embarrassingly long, drawn

out, bout of butt kissing. They were just clothes, there wasn't a need for Anton to debase himself for them. Especially on my behalf, as I wouldn't appreciate the garments enough to make up for the man's wounded pride.

Mr. Silva practically glowed from the praise by the time I grew bored and lightly cleared my throat.

"...and his Grace would look amazing in the new style you come up with for his coronation," Anton looked over at my interruption. "Of course, your Grace, my apologies."

"No, no. It is quite alright, Mr. Kos," I said. "But, I'm sure Mr. Silva's time is very valuable."

"Undoubtedly, your Grace," Anton turned back to Silva. "What do you think? Can you do it?"

Silva cupped his chin and drummed his fingers against his lips before answering, "I could do it, but it would be prohibitively expensive. Almost ruinous. What colors are you thinking?"

Anton looked over to me for guidance. "Do you embroider, or do you send that work to someone else?" I asked.

"I do my own work," Silva clapped his hands sharply. "But, I love that idea!" He shook his finger at me, "It'll cut down the time to finish the job massively. I have the perfect person for the job. What is your design?"

"A Phoenix, wings spread, holding a rose in its beak, talons gripping an orb. Phoenix in red, the rose in black, and a silver orb."

"Oh, how majestic, I love it! Color of the fabrics?"

"Three sets of formal robes, each different. White, with black and red trim. Red, with black trim. And a set of layered red and white, with black trim."

Silva fanned his face, "I think you will look fabulous in those colors."

"For more casual wear, I will defer to your expertise, but would ask that the different items be interchangeable."

"You are just full of good ideas today! Any more and I'll start owing you money!"

"Tie dye."

The bell on the door jingled.

"What?" Mr. Silva asked me, but the potential customer seemed to take offense at his tone.

"How dare you, you immoral peacock! You take that tone with me and I will have you flogged!" A voice I recognized yelled out.

Silva sputtered and the fear in his eyes was real. I stepped in front of him, "Lady Minerva. Have you spoken to Sergeant Park yet? I heard he desperately wanted to ask you some questions."

"You!" Minerva fairly shrieked. "You cost me one hundred Crowns with your lie about being a Duke."

I started to take my gloves off.

"You will pay me back every penny, or I will have the flesh whipped, from, your? Back?"

She had a very similar, shocked reaction, that Sergeant Park had to my mark. Maybe they were related?

"My name is Daniel Hawthorne del Montenegro, Duke of Montenegro."

Everyone in the room bowed. Lady Minerva followed suit, after a beat, and held it longer than the others.

"Your Grace, my apologies for my behavior. My mother often laments my pigheaded behavior."

I nodded to her.

She rose from her bow and pointed at Silva, "This man though, is a known criminal. His immorality is only tolerated because of his skill with fabrics." She waved her hand about the shop. "I was sent here to inform him that he has two days to finish whatever projects he has currently, and then to vacate the premises."

"The only thing left to finish would be the clothing you ordered, Milady," he said archly. "And you didn't even pay for them. If I didn't know any better, I'd think you were trying to get them for free."

"Be careful what you say to me, menos. My mother is not here to protect you."

"But I am," I said.

Minerva narrowed her eyes at me. "We would never miss the Duke we never had," she said as she began to raise her hand.

I didn't want to kill her. I would if I had to, but the political ramifications made me try a spell I hadn't quite perfected yet.

The spell circle jumped into being and conclusion almost at the same time. Purple runes lit the room from corner to corner and I said the activation phrase, "Cleanse."

An indigo aura enveloped Minerva and she yelped, "What?"

Her clothes dissolved and rapidly dissipated. Her hair followed very soon after. All her hair.

Minerva screamed in horror as she ran her hands over her bald scalp, then her face. She looked odd without eyebrows and lashes. She covered her breasts with one arm, her genitals with her other hand, and ran crying from the shop.

Anton buried his face in his hands.

"What just happened?" Silva asked.

"That, is a spell I've been working on," I said. "I still need to tweak it a bit for it to work correctly."

"You mean it wasn't supposed to," he made an up and down gesture with his hand. "All that?"

"Not as such. I wanted a way to cleanse the body and hair, not of hair," I used his same gesture. "I don't know how to go about leaving clothing out at a minimum, or cleaning them as well in a best case scenario."

He nodded along sagely, "I have no idea. I'm not a wizard, but I'd been told that you can't make up spells as you go."

"I have nowhere else to get them," I said. "So if I want to do something with magic, then I need to make it myself."

"Huh," Silva shook himself. "Let's get you measured up and you can tell me all about this tie dye."

So I explained about scrunched up cloth, dye patterns, and rinsing while he measured my arms and legs.

I was surprised I didn't have to disrobe though.

Silva said, "Not worth the trouble."

Sergeant Park burst into the shop as Anton finished paying

the tailor our initial deposit.

"What did you do to my cousin!" Park shouted. He'd entered alone.

Captain Jur waved for Lord Jellinek to take his turn at getting measured before drawing his sword and advancing on the Sergeant.

"If you ruin the cloth with blood, you pay for it!" Silva shouted out, paused for a moment, then looked at me. "Unless you have a way to fix that?"

I guess I could make hydrogen peroxide, it wouldn't be all that difficult. I shook my head though, as I didn't want to be the only source for it, and couldn't come up with any more uses for the stuff that would be worth my time.

Sergeant Park stopped as he heard Silva mention blood. He went pale as he saw Jur bearing down on him and took a step back.

Park held up his hands placatingly, "I'm sorry, your Grace." Sergeant Park bowed low. "I was uncouth."

Jur looked over to me. I shrugged, "I am willing to forgive you this time. Though, if you continue harassing me and mine, an example must be made." I gestured to the door. "Your cousin lives. She will recover fully with time," I shook my head. "The next time it will be her life that she loses. I do not leave enemies to nip at my heels and stab me in the back."

I looked to Jur, "Captain, thank you." Turning back to Park I asked, "Will that be all Sergeant?"

"Uhm yes, your Grace," Sergeant Park yanked at the door and threw himself out the door.

We finished up with Silva quickly after that. And he promised to get our items ready as quickly as possible.

"If you are interested in a patron, then you may consider this a test of your skills. You would be my personal tailor. Which would have you moving to the capital with me."

"I would be honored, your Grace," he paused for a moment, clearly looking uncomfortable. "You, don't mind…" He gestured to himself in an all encompassing way.

"So long as your preferences don't include children or the unwilling," I looked at him pointedly. "Then I don't care what you get up to in your private time. You will have the ear of a Duke, use that power wisely."

We left Silva deep in thought.

A few blocks later Anton asked quietly, "You truly don't care, about…?"

"Hmm? Oh, that. No. It doesn't bother me," I was tempted to tease him, but while I liked Anton, I didn't have that kind of relationship with him.

I smiled sadly, "I can change the law, but I can't change people. You understand?"

Anton cleared his throat, "Of course, your Grace. Thank you."

"Not at all my friend. So where to next?"

Anton seemed grateful for the change of subject, "Lodging for the night, your Grace. They have here in Plav, what is known as a hotel."

"Very well, let's go check it out."

The Plav Hotel didn't look any more impressive from the outside than any other building in Plav. I could start to see why the citizens here dressed the way they did with the dreary construction. The interior was decorated with gilded white marble statues, and colorful tapestries and rugs.

We made our way to the front desk and Anton took care of our accommodations with the man behind the counter. He gave us directions to the bar area while we waited for our rooms to be readied.

I looked to Anton and said, "Do me a favor and find me all the information on this place you can."

"Of course, your Grace. Anything in particular?"

"Who owns it, who runs it, how many they have, are they interested in a partner or in having competition?"

"I see. I'll see to it, Milord."

"Thank you, Mr. Kos," I nodded to him.

Ten minutes later, we were escorted to our rooms on the third floor. They were nice rooms with big beds and a working toilet, which was really impressive for the level of technology seen here before inTallinn. That was going off of earth's history. Without the Dark age choke-hold, the Roman Catholic church, had in Europe, different technologies could have advanced much faster here.

Some of the fashions had an Asian feel, but gunpowder didn't seem to be a thing. Magic ability would keep certain things from being practical, and make others obsolete.

I turned on the tap for the bath and tested the warm water, it was just right. I had the whole suite to myself so I disrobed, then got comfortable and clean until dinner.

The next few days went by without any major incidents. Messages were sent ahead of us to the capitol, a branch office of the Bank registered to open here in Plav, and everything was running to schedule.

Silva sent a note informing us the clothes would be ready in two more days. Our merchants were doing brisk business within the city, and our mercenaries were, for the most part, staying out of trouble.

There were rumors of trouble in the borderlands. Binsar soldiers raided across the border, stole some livestock, and maybe, no one was too sure, burned a barn or two. That didn't sound like a prelude to invasion, so I put it off for a bit while I consolidated my power.

Goblin activity was reported as sporadic across the Duchy. The people were used to a heavier presence of the pests and were happy about the change in habits. I'd need more concrete data, but the trend indicated a migration, where to or why I couldn't say. Something else to put on the back burner.

"Really, your Grace, it should be a priority to you," Anton admonished me. "Political power follows dynastic families. People like stability. Knowing the kind of people who will be in charge is important for that stability."

"Idiots are born into positions of power all the time."

"They are also elected all the time, if your stories are to be believed."

"Fair enough," I sighed. "But, I don't have anything to wear to a ball."

Anton held up a garment bag before I finished my sentence. "You will look dashing, your Grace."

I gave him a sour look, "I am not getting married tonight."

"Very good, Milord," Anton nodded affably. "Wait until after the church anoints you. That way you will have been confirmed as the head of your own House," Anton gave the bag a little shake and me a smug look. "That way they are marrying into your family, not the other way around."

"Who is hosting the ball? And is there really dancing or is it just a bunch of people standing around talking politics?"

"The Lancaster family is hosting. Sometimes yes, sometimes no. I am not from Montenegro so some of their customs do come as a surprise. Mostly it is the younger people who enjoy dancing. The women with power view these events as work and treat it as such"

"Very well, Mr. Kos. Let's see what Mr. Silva sent over."

Anton pulled the garment bag that covered the clothes, revealing the robes underneath. The robe itself was red with black trim and embroidery. My Phoenix motif stood on the left breast, cuffs, and back; each sized appropriately. The shirt and pants were a soft pale cream.

"Don't forget the slippers, your Grace," Anton said with far too much mirth.

The moccasins, I refused to call them slippers, were red with black stitching, and hard soles. They weren't bad, per say, but

I'd rather wear my boots. I took the clothes and the footwear from him.

"Thank you, Mr. Kos. I will get ready now," I began to turn away then had a thought. "Would you arrange transport, to and from the venue, for us?"

"Us, your Grace?" Anton asked with a slight frown.

"Of course. You wouldn't have me go without my chaperone, would you?"

It was Anton's turn to sigh, "I would never, Milord. I will see to it at once, your Grace."

"Thank you, Mr. Kos," I turned and placed the clothing on the bed.

Chapter 16

Compared to all the other overdressed peacocks here, I looked good. I definitely stood out from the crowd as my attire wasn't eye jarring, and headache inducing.

Robes, dresses, and gowns abounded. Some even wore pants, though no clothing seemed to be gender specific. Everyone wore clashing colors, like someone broke open a piñata and turned on a fan.

Boys and girls romped around in their finery, chaperones chasing after them. Teens grouped up and divided based on sex, boys on the left of the dance floor and girls on the right. The men mingled on the dance floor. But, not dancing, they seemed to be gossiping, shooting looks in different directions. Most of them my way. I ignored them.

The women sat at various tables with varied drinks to hand and plates of victuals before them. Anton and I stood well off to the side. No one approached us as of yet. Not even the servers who flitted about the place.

"It would seem, Mr. Kos, that I am being ostracized," I smirked at him. "Put in my place, if you will."

"Your Grace, I do wish you would take this seriously."

I gestured to the crowd of people, drawing some more eyes our way. I pointed a finger, for dramatic effect, at a passing tray with what looked to be glasses of whiskey. Flowers etched into the sides of the vessels made the amber liquid sparkle within. Two beverages floated over to us, dodging a pair of teens who weren't paying attention, and into my hands. I handed one to Anton, to various real and fake gasps, from the attendees.

One fellow started so badly he upended his glass of wine over the head of the man beside him. He, of course, apologized profusely and explained loudly that it was all my fault for causing a scene. That the pourer had to reach up to pour the drink over the taller gentleman was beside the point.

"Not in your wildest dreams, my friend," I laughed softly.

"Ahem," sounded behind me.

I turned to find a very lovely lady in purple, orange, and yellow. Her skirt alternated between purple and orange while her blouse was yellow. Dark ringlets cascaded over her shoulders and framed her pretty face. She looked a little mischievous with the twinkle in her light brown eyes.

"Are you quite done causing trouble, your Grace?" She sounded more amused than irritated.

I gave her a half bow, that Anton assured me earlier, would not offend.

"Probably not," I smiled. "If only I had someone to keep me

occupied and out of trouble." I turned back to the crowd of onlookers. "But, alas, no one seems like they want to speak with me."

"Really?" I saw her look pointedly at Anton out of the corner of my eye.

I raised my glass to take a sip. And almost spit out the apple juice. I set the glass in the air to let it hover off to my side.

The lady covered her mouth to hide her smile; it couldn't hide her tinkling laughter. "Not what you were expecting my Lord?"

I heaved an exaggerated sigh, "Not at all, my Lady. Though, it seems as if I am invisible to every server who passes by. It would be an amazing ability, if I'd actually intended to use it as such."

She giggled behind her hand again. The demure behavior was attractive, but this culture didn't support it, and it made me suspicious. Almost everyone in the ballroom watched us.

I cut a glance at Anton, he just looked worried. One of the older women seated at a table smirked at me. She reminded me of Minerva.

I sent a wink her way and she frowned.

I glanced back at the lady in front of me. "Did you hear what happened to Lady Minerva the other day?" I asked loudly.

The woman in front of me gasped, "Oh, tell me you know something! No one will speak of it!"

The obvious relative of Minerva stood abruptly, I continued anyway.

"Yes. She offended a higher ranked noble, and as punishment, they cast a spell to clean her right up."

The other woman, who I'd guess to be an aunt, stalked closer.

"What kind of spell? What did it do?"

"Well," I said deprecatingly. "It's a work in progress, meant to clean a person." I leaned forward like I had a secret though I didn't lower my voice, "But, it removed everything. Oil, dirt, clothing." The lady gasped, and I went on, "Hair, and any other contaminants she had on her."

I shuddered for effect, "Absolutely ghastly, what a person looks like without eyebrows!"

The lady covered her face, "Oh no! How horrible!"

"Yes," I turned to face the oncoming woman as she stopped before me. "She shouldn't have attacked the Duke with a spell. She really is lucky to have lived through the experience."

I turned my attention back to the now pale lady, "It is always a good idea to know the depth of the waters before you jump in head first."

I turned back to the older woman, "Don't you agree…"

"Lady Shannon, my Lord," she scowled at me.

I turned to Anton and he said, "His Grace, my Lady."

"What?"

"The way to properly address a Duke is, your or his, Grace. My lady."

"You mean this imposter? I will throw this trash out myself."

She didn't give me a chance to take my gloves off before her lance of fire struck my hasty shield. I mentally shoved Anton away to keep him safe. Shannon sent a dozen arrows of fire trying to bypass my defense. No longer surprised, I simply widened out my shield to catch all the projectiles.

"What is the meaning of this!" A voice shouted out.

Shannon paused in her next attack, and I struck during the opening, with a volley of my Arcane Bolts. If she had a shield of her own up, it didn't show, as my six bolts plowed right into her, lifted her from her feet, and threw her several meters away to lay still on the floor.

The sound of many feet slapping the floor approached, and I turned my attention to them. Guards began to surround me with swords drawn. Anton threw a handful of Marks and Crowns to me. I caught them in my telekinetic grip and had them orbit around me.

My mana sense kept tabs on the men that surrounded me, by noting the swirls and patterns they made on the ambient mana while breathing. One man behind me made to move forward, only to topple over stiffly.

"Stand down now!" The same voice from before shouted, startling two men in front of me, which made two others lunge forward to fall on their faces.

Anton threw more coins to land at my feet. The men around me took a step back as they noticed the coins join the others around me.

A wall of wind blew the gathered men away from me. I could feel it beating against my shield, indicating that the spell was indiscriminate at the very least. At least the immediate threat was removed.

"Lady Lancaster, stay back!" Shannon yelled from the floor as she struggled to her knees. "He's an animal!"

"His Grace, is here at my invitation, and the next person to attack him will die," a matronly woman with gray hair stepped over one of the dead guards.

I put my index finger to the tip of my nose and then pointed to her. Her forceful march stuttered as she missed a step.

Lady Shannon stood up on shaky legs, her face ugly with rage, as she pointed at me. Lancaster noticed my gaze and spun in place to see the fire die in Shannon's hand as she stiffened and fell. Her left foot twitched a few times then stilled. The quiet in the ballroom was absolute.

I moved over to Anton and asked, "Are you alright?"

"I'm fine, your Grace," Anton's eyes searched me. "Never mind me, are you injured?"

"Me? I was never in danger."

Several guests gasped and a man fainted, falling onto a servant's tray of wine glasses, causing a crash of broken glass to cascade across the dance floor.

Lady Lancaster approached me cautiously, "Your Grace, I humbly apologize for the attack on your person."

She knelt down and bowed with her head to the floor. I patted Anton on the shoulder and nodded when he looked at me.

"Like last time, your Grace?"

I nodded, letting Anton be my Voice in this matter.

Anton looked down at Lady Annette Lancaster, head of House Lancaster, Baroness of Plav, and all round nice lady most of the time. She wasn't truly at fault for what happened here. But, it was her House, and her honor at stake.

"Lady Annette Lancaster, His Grace, the Duke of Montenegro and your direct liege, holds you blameless in this instance. You intervened as soon as Lady Shannon attacked on, his Grace's behalf. You told her guards, of which she was the only noble to bring them, to stand down. You also instructed Lady Shannon herself to stop, which she ignored, before you used your magic to safeguard the participants."

Anton looked around at the gathered nobles, of which all had eyes as wide as saucers, "Are there any members of the peerage here that dispute this judgment and claims?"

Anton waited several heartbeats before stating, "You must speak out now, or never. To be forever branded a coward if one is to offer up a different opinion as to what has happened here today. The honor of Lady Lancaster will not be impinged upon because your own honor is lacking, here and now."

I had to still my face to keep from smirking. Anton laid it on pretty thick, and enjoyed himself thoroughly. He waited several minutes, giving anyone present ample time to gather their thoughts and courage.

"Rise Lady Lancaster, be recognized by your liege, and stand with honor, knowing his Grace stands with you."

Lady Lancaster stood on her own, a little wobbly perhaps, but under her own power, to the applause of those gathered. I gave her a half bow, and extended my elbow to her. She glanced at Anton then smiled up at me as she hooked her arm in mine.

"I've never seen that done before," she whispered.

"You're doing great," I leaned down and whispered back.

She patted my arm and said aloud, "Well, maybe we can start a new fade amongst the children."

I led her over to the nearest table, going around the body of Shannon on our way there. I pulled her seat out for her and she nodded her thanks. As she sat, I waved over one of the servants, and when he came over, handed Lady Lancaster a glass of wine. I took one for myself and sat across from her. We studied one another as we sipped, neither one wanting to speak first.

Anton came and bowed to Baroness Lancaster, "My Lady, may I formally introduce you to his Grace, Duke Daniel del Montenegro, first of his House."

Annette Lancaster rose gracefully and bowed formally. I rose as well and gave her a half bow. I thought all this bowing excessive, but Anton lectured me at great length, about how the customs of my people were more important than my own preconceived notions.

"Your Grace, be welcomed to my home," she gestured, out of habit it seemed, because she grimaced over at the bodies strewn about. "Or at least more welcome than the reception you have already seen."

I waved her comment away, "I was prepared for something to happen tonight." I leaned forward like I had a secret, "Though if I'm honest, I thought I'd be assaulted by the lovely lady who approached me first."

Annette sat up quickly with wide eyes. "Annice? What did she do?" Lady Lancaster looked about searching for the younger woman.

I smiled, "Nothing, but be a charming young woman. I wasn't prepared for such a cordial greeting."

"Oh, thank the goddess!" She gave up looking around and focused back on me. "She's a sweet girl. I couldn't imagine my granddaughter acting that way on her own." Annette leaned forward, copying my posture, "The gift skipped her, so she's been more of a follower, than the leader she should be."

I nodded along and let my disappointment show. "That is a shame. She was quite lovely, and a delight to speak with."

Annette cocked her head to the side, "Why a shame, your Grace? I don't understand."

Anton took a half step forward. Some of these courting customs were downright odd. "Lady Lancaster, his Grace, is looking to match with a woman with specific traits. The inborn gift being one of them."

"Oh dear," Annette sat back thoughtfully then turned to look toward a group of teens. The oldest might, with a slim possibility, be sixteen.

"Over the age of eighteen," I blurted out.

Annette let her half-raised hand fall to her side and looked at me incredulously. "Why would you do that to yourself?" She continued before I could answer. "You reduce your pool of eligible partners by almost ninety percent!"

"His Grace is most adamant. Not only has he required an age range, and magical ability, but all prospects must also be without children of their own," Anton nodded to her look of disbelief. "In the case of the woman having 'known the touch of a man,' a one year betrothal is-"

"That is preposterous!" Lady Lancaster stood abruptly, her chair clattered as it fell to the floor. "Most noble women have had their first man by fourteen! And a child by sixteen if they're incredibly unlucky."

She shook her finger at me, "If you don't wish to wed then say so! At least have the balls to be honest about your intentions."

Anton took a step back, shocked at the Lady's outburst. I gave her a gentle smile and spoke softly, "If I removed the requirement of noble birth, I could find a wife by tomorrow."

The servant who righted Annette's chair did so with impeccable timing as the woman collapsed into the newly placed chair.

"You wouldn't!" She asked in a strangled whisper.

My smile turned to a smirk, "Lady Lancaster, I would expect that the behavior of my nobles, who lead my people, would be above reproach." I sat back in my chair, "Have you seen the Dome of Risin, my Lady?"

"But, but the church of Mithira preaches…" She trailed off, suddenly understanding my position.

I nodded to her and smiled, "I will, of course, stay with the custom of marrying a daughter of an established House. Too much push back, and I will simply raise a farmer's family into the nobility, then marry their daughter."

Her mouth dropped open and the blood drained from her face. The idea truly horrified her. "Please," she whimpered. "No, Goddess, no."

I tilted my head back and looked down on her, "Montenegro's past nobles exterminated the House of her last Duke. Are you so shocked that I don't come from an old line?"

"No, your Grace," Annette grabbed her wine roughly, spilling some on her wrist, and drained the rest.

When she caught her breath she said, "Your Grace, the Goddess Herself, chose you. No one worth their salt would question your suitability. But, a commoner, not so chosen?" She motioned with her empty wine glass to a servant, her hand visibly shaking.

"Well, your granddaughter is a truly lovely lady, and I'm sorry a match couldn't be made here tonight," I said.

"Of course, your Grace," Annette gave me a weak smile. "I see your point clearly."

The same man who'd been serving Annette placed a glass unobtrusively on the table and started to move away, but I telekinetically snagged his sleeve before he could disappear. He turned to me wide-eyed and asked in a quivering voice, "Yes, your Grace?"

I gave him my most disarming smile, that made sweat pop out on his brow, and asked, "Do you happen to have any distilled beverages about? Preferably made with grains?"

"Of course, your Grace?" The servant frowned. "Any grain in particular? Barley, hops, or corn?"

I let out a happy sigh. "Corn. Please," I stopped him from leaving again. "One moment, if you will?"

He nodded, nervous again.

"First," I held up a finger and he nodded. "Get someone, who is not handling food and drinks, to clean up the mess in here," he nodded.

"Secondly," I held up two fingers. "Bring me samples of each grain alcohol you have with labels."

He looked confused, but nodded along.

"Lastly," I put my hand down. "After the clean up is done, and the musicians begin, please bring me some food." He nodded. "Any questions?" He shook his head. "Excellent! Thank you."

He bowed, then ran away. Not, he walked briskly. Or with celerity. He sprinted away, arms pumping, feet thumping against the floor, running.

Annette giggled then covered her mouth when she saw me look at her. I could see where her granddaughter got her charm from.

"Edward means well," she defended the man. "But, he doesn't handle pressure well. He likes to remain in the background."

I looked over to the man in question. He gestured to some guards, to the floor, and to me. His mouth moved a mile a minute, and when a guard shook his head, Edward grew more forceful.

I smiled at Annette, "You might be surprised. Give him a

chance and I'm sure he'll surprise you."

"You don't," Annette coughed. "Fancy him, do you?"

I gave her my best, 'are you fucking kidding,' look.

She at least had the decency to blush.

"Well, the rumors ran faster than Minerva from Silva's shop," Annette said through pouting lips as she crossed her thin arms.

Music started up, soft and uncertain, accompanied by the low chatter of furious whispers.

Annette's mouth dropped open and she leaned forward to whisper incredulously, "How did you know they would stay after the fight?"

"Several reasons," I didn't bother to whisper. "Everyone here is involved in politics in one way or another, so they just have to know what happens next. By returning their sense of normalcy, not panicking, and cleaning up, their fear is controlled. Most people seek leadership." I gestured broadly, "If you seem in charge, like you know what you're doing, then they will follow you. Perception becomes reality." I gave her a small bow from my seat.

Clapping from behind startled me and I raised a glowing shield that lit up a frightened Edward and a woman who looked shocked as well. I canceled my spell immediately and the clear aura around both of them disappeared.

"My apologies, your Grace," the raven haired woman said with a bow. "I didn't think my actions through, in light of recent events. Please forgive me."

"Of course milady," I said, trying to keep my poise. "Will you be joining us?" I hoped so as I strongly suspected that hers and Edward's aura was an indication for them to lack an affinity. If I understood correctly, then most tests for gifted individuals wouldn't pick them up.

"If you don't mind, after my rudeness?" She gave an apologetic smile.

I waved her to a chair between Annette and I at the oval table. Edward set glassware and bottles on the table before me.

"Ladies?" I waved my hand expensively at the libations before me. "Would you care to join me?"

Annette shook her head, "No thank you, your Grace. I never acquired the taste for the distilled drinks." She looked at the other woman. "Lady Margaret, surely you won't make the Duke drink alone?"

Margaret paled, though she got Annette's point immediately. I would not be drinking alone.

"Excellent!" I pretended not to notice the power play going on in front of me. "Edward, please tell me about the beverages you have for us, as you pour them."

"Of course, your Grace," he bowed before selecting an unlabeled green bottle.

"Mr. Kos," I looked over my shoulder to him. "Will you be joining us?"

Anton narrowed his eyes at me, "Regretfully not, your Grace. As your chaperone, it is incumbent upon me to retain my wits."

"Ah. Of course, of course," I grinned broadly at him. "More for me!" I heard him sigh as I turned back to the table. Annette, as matronly as she was, giggled at the byplay. I gave Edward my attention as he poured a splash into my glass.

"I have the honor, your Grace, to present to you a distilled malt barley, aged one hundred fifty years in a charred oak barrel. 'Williams' is a very reputable distiller of fine whiskey."

Margaret and I raised our glasses to one another, though she seemed to rethink her decision to join my table.

The whiskey burned from my throat to my stomach, and left a pleasant warmth after the initial shock. The aftertaste was of smoked vanilla and tannin. I smacked my lips several times. Margaret's eyes bulged slightly, but she kept it down.

"Next, your Grace?" Edward asked.

"But of course, my good man," I gave an exaggerated gesture to him. "You have only begun to wet my appetite!" I said unnecessarily loud.

"Very good, your Grace," he poured from a brown bottle with a green label that his hand covered. "Next we have a fifty-five percent rye with added barley and corn. Made by Countess Danielle Ambrose, this particular bottle is a one of twenty-five limited edition, aged ten years in red oak."

The amber whiskey had a robust and strong scent of caramel. The burn of the alcohol blended well with the peppery taste. Margaret, to no surprise, turned a rather interesting shade of green.

"Clench your teeth and breathe through your mouth," I leaned over and whispered.

She immediately took my advice and her color returned to normal.

Edward looked at me with his eyebrow raised. I shook my head and asked, "Maybe some water to cleanse our palates?"

"At once, your Grace," he raised two fingers to shoulder height and then recorked the bottle.

Two tall glasses and a glass pitcher full of water were placed on the table. Edward nodded to the servant and poured Margaret and I a glass each. I sipped while Margaret gulped hers down with gusto.

"Lady Margaret, would you rather have some wine?" I asked.

"If you wouldn't mind, your Grace."

"Well, I have one more bottle to taste before I make my selection, as I don't favor wine myself. But," I nodded to her. "You drink what you like. Forcing yourself to drink whiskey you don't like won't impress me."

"Thank you for your kindness, your Grace," she turned to Edward. "A dry red."

Edward held up a finger then made a swirling motion with a dip at the end. "It will be but a moment, my Lady."

A few moments later a glass of red wine was placed before Margaret.

"Shall we continue, Mr. Edward?" I asked.

"As you wish, your Grace." The third, and final bottle Edward grabbed, was clear without a label, setting the light amber fluid on full display.

"This whiskey is made of over sixty percent corn, and aged for ten years in oak barrels. The honorable Raegon family has made this particular recipe for over three hundred years. They are the oldest consecutive family distillery in Montenegro. This particular recipe was said to be favored by Osvaldo himself, our former Duke."

Annette and Margaret stiffened and went pale. I merely smiled and said, "Let's see if the man had good taste then!"

Edward bowed to me and poured a splash into my glass. Both ladies mirrored one another by sighing.

The whiskey didn't have the alcohol content of the rye, and was smoother than the malt barley. It warmed pleasantly with a butter toffee and vanilla finish. Old Osvaldo had good taste in whiskey.

"Mr. Edward, I also favor the Raegon," I nodded to the bottle. "Two fingers, if you please."

"An excellent choice, your Grace." He grabbed a new glass, held it up for my inspection, and poured my drink when I nodded. He slid the amber whiskey over to me.

I dipped two fingers into my water then let three drops of water fall into my drink. I would sip my ambrosia for my remaining time here.

Edward went to fade into the background once again, when Lady Lancaster snagged his sleeve and whispered severely at him. His face paled and his shoulders took on a dejected air. I waved at Anton and nodded to Edward. Anton gave me a firm nod in return. Edward removed the used and finished bottles and glasses to his tray and left. Anton surreptitiously followed. Good man.

A light cough caught the attention of the women at the table. I continued to enjoy my first whiskey in years. Amanda didn't like it, or the smell of it, so she demanded I not drink it. I'd gone along with her demand, thinking to make her happy. It didn't work.

"Your Grace," Annette got my attention. "May I introduce to you, Mayor Plana Papic."

"Madame Mayor," I said and nodded to her.

She gave a slight bow and smirked. I simply raised an eyebrow. Plana's brow furrowed, then she straightened and she placed some papers before me.

I looked at Annette, but her severe frown deepened the already deep lines on her face.

"What do we have here, Madame Mayor?" I asked.

"Titles that need ratification. Your Grace," her pause was obvious. "It is simply a formality at this point as the lands were sold long ago."

"So why involve me then?" I took a sip from my glass. "If you," I paused and looked her in the eye. "It was you, yes?"

She looked a little uncertain now. "Yes, your Grace."

I nodded, "Then if you had the authority to sell these lands," I flipped through the paperwork, noting that they were supposed to be lands held in trust. Meaning she didn't have the authority to sell or dispose of these properties. "Then you don't need me to sign anything."

"But, Baroness Gretchen bought these properties ten years ago."

"You sold land to this woman? My land?"

"Yes, your Grace. But, it is much too late to do anything about it now, like I said."

"It wasn't yours to sell. Your family held it in trust," I leaned forward. "To manage the land. They had no legal right to sell it."

I sat back, scratched my beard, and thought for a moment.

"I'll let it stand as a lease with a one year extension. After that we can negotiate a rental term, or depending on her behavior, an execution."

"But… Her family is very powerful. Most of the land they own-"

"Was never theirs in the first place," I interrupted. "Madame Mayor, I'm willing to deal honestly with them, but things will not be as they were. If they insist on keeping their criminal holdings then they can go to the gallows."

Mayor Papic sat, visibly pale, and looked to the women on either side of her for help. Both noblewomen avoided meeting her gaze.

"This, this is ridiculous!" the Mayor shouted. She flinched back from the glares her outburst engendered.

She didn't seem to understand.

"Your Grace," Anton asked from behind Plana. "Is there another problem?

Annette shot to her feet, Margaret right behind her, and said firmly, "There is not. She will keep a civil tongue in her head, or I will have it removed."

"You? What?" Plana sputtered.

"I had no part in this," Annette said.

I handed the papers to Anton, who looked them over quickly. Edward I noted stood three steps behind him.

"Some of these properties are here in the city," Anton looked up at the women then addressed me. "Others are in the capital, with a smattering throughout the Duchy."

I focused fully on the Mayor, "It will be your responsibility to inform Lady Gretchen, as soon as possible mind you, of the situation. Starting with the properties here in Plav."

"See if one of those here would be a suitable residence for me," I said over my shoulder.

The Mayor swayed on her feet. "This can't be happening," Plana said to herself.

Annette slapped the Mayor in the face. "Get a hold of yourself! Obviously the Duke won't ratify the sale of his properties. The only thing left to do is exactly what he said. Do not embarrass your family anymore than you already have."

Anton slid a paper in front of me. "This one is across the street from here, your Grace," he said to my questioning look.

I turned back to the Mayor, "You'll want to start there. I find I'm tired of staying at the hotel. I'd like a place of my own."

Plana Papic fell like a puppet with its strings cut.

Chapter 17

I stretched out in my new bed. I lucked out with the property being vacant. I'd have felt bad for evicting someone, just so I could make a political statement, and be a little more comfortable. It wasn't too different from the hotel, though anyone who has vacationed in a house versus a hotel, just knows. The level of privacy is magnificent, not that I needed it, but it is nice to have.

My coronation was coming up soon, I'd toyed with the idea of waiting for my one year anniversary in this world to have it.

That kind of correlation would've been lost on most of my people, and definitely worried my nobles. I'd have needed to wait four more months anyway.

I took care of my morning ablutions and made my way downstairs to an amazing omelet that Sin-Nasir said he, "threw together," which I highly doubted. So after an amazing breakfast, I waved Anton over from where he waited with Edward at the entryway to the dining room.

Anton sat down with a stack of papers while Edward stood unobtrusively against the wall.

"What do you have for me this morning, Mr. Kos?" In as grandiose and magnanimous a manner as I could. I wanted to share my good mood.

"Execution orders, your Grace," Anton said heavily. "I am sorry to ruin your good cheer, but these are last minute appeals to you as the highest authority in the Duchy."

"No, I understand," I sighed. "Let's go through them so that justice may be served."

We went through the different cases one by one all morning. I didn't have to be as thorough, but in a case of life-or-death, my due diligence was the least I could give.

In the end, I confirmed all, except two cases. One, where a young noble woman accused a man of forfeiting a marriage contract. She was juggling several different men and wanted James, the accused, to help pressure the man she did want. James, a minor noble, ended up poisoned and missed the wedding.

The second worried me though. A young peasant boy was splashing his way through mud puddles following his father's produce cart, when a noble woman stepped between the cart and the child. Mud splashed the woman, who crossed the street without looking, and blamed the child. She cast fire at the boy, but the father lunged between them, and blocked the flames from the boy. In his lunge, while on fire, the father tackled the noble woman, and set her alight. Both died from their injuries.

The boy was being charged with recklessness, and ultimately blamed for the whole incident. I made sure to dismiss all charges on the boy, fined the noble family who prosecuted the child, and accused the magistrate of corruption with an investigation to follow.

Edward looked shocked at my reaction. "Your Grace, why would you side with a peasant over one of your nobles? You have just made an enemy of someone with power."

"You don't think commoners have power, Edward?" I looked at Anton, "Mr. Kos, how many landed nobles are in my Duchy?"

"There are one hundred registered landed nobles, your Grace, as of the last census."

I nodded, "And, of commoners?"

Anton smiled, "With many lacking the ability to count, the number is unsure, but ten to thirty thousand is the best guess, your Grace."

I turned back to Edward, "You see? Even unarmed and untrained they pose a formidable force." I shook my head, "Given enough motivation, a cause to rally around, like a child given the death penalty over splashed mud, and even the most powerful noble would be slaughtered in their homes."

Edward nodded slowly, as though the thought had never occurred to him. "I see, your Grace. Thank you for the explanation."

"Of course," I waved him over to the table and gestured to a chair beside me. "Now that that unpleasantness is out of the way, I have some questions for you."

Edward hurried over and sat abruptly, his full attention on me.

"You were tested for magic?" He nodded, though his forehead scrunched up.

"You were told you lacked an affinity?" He nodded the same as before.

"Would you learn diligently, and study hard, if you were given the opportunity?" His eyes widened and he rocked back as if struck.

"Your Grace, I would," he shook his head. "But, I've been told it is impossible."

I smiled at him, "It is possible, though I would need an oath from you before we go any further."

"You have it!" He nearly shouted at me. "I swear, by holy Mithira, that nothing you say will ever pass these lips. May my tongue be torn from its roots before the words pass them."

An Arcane glow surrounded Edward, sealing his oath.

"Very well, thank you, Edward." I put my elbows on the table and steepled my fingers. "It is possible to teach you. You will need to choose the affinity you want the most. It is a choice that can not be unmade."

"I can choose Water?" He asked, awed.

I grinned at him, "That easy huh?"

"What would you have of me, your Grace?" Hope shone in his eyes.

"Your service, and fealty, to my family, forevermore," the grin fell from my face.

"I vow to serve you, your Grace, and the Montenegro family,

for my entire life, or until released from your service. May the Mother of Mysteries hear and mark my Vow."

Edward sucked in a breath through his teeth as the same mark Anton had, and a Phoenix, formed on his hand.

"Excellent," I took the proffered stack of notebooks from Anton, and leafed through them. I selected the Water affinity basics and slid it over to Edward. "This is on loan to you. Master these spells, if you still wish to continue learning, based on your service, I will help you more."

Edward took the guide book reverently.

"The beginning of the guide tells you how to manipulate mana," I kept eye contact with him. "I highly suggest that you spend some extra time going through those exercises."

"Thank you, your Grace," Edward got up, knelt on the floor, and pressed his forehead to the floor. "This means more to me than I can ever say."

I really wish they could just say thank you. Like normal people. I was starting to get used to the bowing. They used it like a handshake. But, this made me uncomfortable in a way I hope I never get used to.

"I might surprise you, Edward. Please, rise," I waited until he was back on his feet. "I understand how exciting this can be, but please, don't let Mr. Kos down by neglecting your other duties."

He glanced over at Anton, "I will do as Mr. Kos instructed, your Grace."

"Excellent. We will, of course, place you according to your new talents when they emerge."

"Thank you, your Grace," he took that as his dismissal and left the dining room.

Anton frowned after him and I chuckled.

"You haven't assigned him anything yet, have you?"

"I wasn't quite sure why you wanted him, your Grace," he looked at me askance. "Though, I'm sure you had your reasons."

"Several, my friend," I ticked them off on my fingers. "I have to keep up appearances. You're much too important to use as a gopher. And he was out of a job doing exactly what I asked him to do."

"A gopher, Milord?" Anton's face looked appalled.

"Yeah, go fur, this. Go fur, that." I smiled widely as he rolled his eyes.

"How very droll, Milord."

I nodded appreciably, "So he can serve as my personal valet.

Pay him more than he was making with Lady Lancaster."

Anton tapped his chin in thought, "And what does a," he looked at me with an eyebrow raised. "You called it a valet?" I nodded. "What does a valet do, exactly?"

"Fetch quests, open doors, run errands, anything that an untrained person can do," I nodded in the general direction of the street. "Our clothes should be ready soon. He'd be the perfect person to go get them." I pressed my tongue to my cheek. "He might need a note."

"A note, Milord?"

"Sure. Mr. Silva might not know him, and won't hand over the order. Then Edward would have to trek all the way back here empty handed," I smirked. "Just to then turn around, and go all the way back, with a note."

"A note is an excellent idea, your Grace," Anton nodded sagely. "Sometimes, one must know when the mouth is best used for chewing."

I nodded along knowingly for a moment, then asked, "Do you have anything else for me today?"

"There is nothing scheduled, your Grace."

"Good," I placed my hands on the table to help push myself up. "In that case I will work on my meditation the rest of the day. Notify me in case of an emergency that you can't handle."

I clapped him on the shoulder, "Otherwise, I'll see you at dinner."

Anton raised an eyebrow, "And if a lady should come calling?"

I shook my head, "Then I'm busy, and they should schedule a time with my chaperone."

"Very good, Milord."

I spent the rest of the day in seclusion. I tried to pack as much mana, as evenly as possible, into my Core as I could. While thick in the air around me, the mana felt like cotton candy as I mentally grasped it. It stuck in clumps; just a general pain in my ass. Meditation was supposed to be relaxing. After several hours, I was a sweaty mess and my body ached like I'd run for miles.

A putrid scent wafted up to me so I checked to see if my Aura of Ambiance was still working. It was. But, the thick sludge that covered my body overpowered my spell. My pants and shirt were ruined, never mind my underwear.

I waddled into my bathroom and started the shower. Peeling the clothes off my body was one of the most disgusting things I've ever done. Luckily the stuff washed off without too much effort. Lye soap was some powerful stuff.

After washing all the gunk out of my beard, I needed to find some lotions and oils to keep it from itching something fierce. Unlike what some people thought, it wasn't the hair growing that made your face itch. The hair steals the moisture from your face, and that makes it itch.

After getting clean and dry, I glanced into the mirror by the wardrobe. I was shocked by what I saw in the reflection. Me, but wholly different. My spare tire was gone. I didn't suddenly have abs now, though with some work, I could definitely see that happening.

My stomach gurgled it's displeasure. Time for dinner, regardless of the time. I put a robe on while I thought about the changes to my body.

Wizards came in all shapes and sizes so this must be an effect of cultivating a Core. It wasn't a big stretch of the imagination to realize how the metaphysical could impact the physical. I could make fire, or move things with my mind, so yeah.

Sin-Nasir wrung his hands as he saw me making a sandwich. Appalled, to come into his kitchen, and find me in there, but after watching me polish off three sandwiches he almost settled down.

I waved a butter knife around as I said, "The secret to a great sandwich isn't what you put into it necessarily." I waved the dull instrument about, "Now I know what you're thinking."

"You couldn't possib-"

I interrupted without acknowledging him, "How can the ingredients not matter?" I nodded to him. "And you're right, to a point. But, the secret is to make every bite taste and feel the same."

I buttered then toasted, the bread I'd sliced from a large round loaf I'd found in my rummaging. I definitely needed to find out how to make mayonnaise. I sliced up a tomato, chicken breast, and some cheddar cheese. Flipped the bread in the pan then moved a few steps to wash the spinach in a basin.

I layered my ingredients between the pieces of bread, then sliced the sandwich in half. I grabbed then took a bite off one half. I chewed while cutting up the other into smaller portions. I handed a small piece to Sin-Nasir. He took it absently and popped it into his mouth. His look became thoughtful as he chewed.

"This could use some mayonnaise," he said.

"I know, right!" I said around a mouthful of sandwich.

"Your Grace," Sin-Nasir said firmly enough to grab my attention. "Have you given thought to my request?"

"To throw a ball?" I asked.

"Yes, your Grace," he smoothed down his apron.

"Yes, I've thought about it," I said.

He waited for me to elaborate, but I continued to enjoy my sandwich. Finally he'd had enough, "Really, your Grace?" He asked exasperated. "Am I not diligent to your needs?"

I held up my sandwich. He threw his hands into the air.

"Dinner will be served in a few hours, I'm sure you could have waited a bit longer."

My stomach decided to rebuff his argument with a loud growl of its own. I grabbed the rest of the cut up sandwich.

"Fine," I said. "You and Anton plan it, and I'll be there," I held up a finger to stop his enthusiasm. "We leave in two weeks for the capital. You will not only have the opportunity, but my every expectation, to make the coronation feast as grand as possible."

If I actually thought that would dampen Sin-Nasir's enthusiasm, I'd have been very wrong. "I would suggest that you hire a staff, and use this banquet as a training opportunity."

"As wise as ever, your Grace," Sin-Nasir bowed in half at the waist. "From your lips to my heart, it will be done."

I nodded and marveled at his eccentricities as I walked away.

"I'll be in the study, please notify me when dinner is served."

"As you wish, your Grace," Sin-Nasir said.

The study contained a heavy oak desk, a couple of brown leather oversized plush chairs, and several book shelves. I spent a while pursuing the book titles on display. Some caught my interest enough to open a few, to see what was inside.

I'd already pushed, pulled, removed, and fondled each book to see if they opened a secret passage. They hadn't, but I haven't given up hope just yet.

I selected a book on rune theory and spell creation. Which is just what the title stated. I learned several new symbols by the time dinner was ready. Just not one that would help my cleanse spell.

Dinner was a dense pasta with a thick, heavy tomato sauce. Spicy sausage cut into coins was sprinkled liberally throughout the dish. Sin-Nasir made sure I didn't leave the table hungry.

Chapter 18

After a week of meditation, learning runes, and expanding my grasp of magic theory, the day of the banquet arrived. I'd finally found the proper symbols for my cleanse spell, though I kept the other as a 'less than lethal' way to deal with someone. Life was cheap in this world, and I could feel my own values change to reflect that. It was disheartening, but if someone insisted on taking my life, to hell with them.

Sin-Nasir created a masterful array of foods for the dinner. A twenty-seven course meal full of salads, meats, soups, pastries, and chocolate desserts. He took my advice and hired twelve helpers, though one woman got fired after the first night. I found her naked in my bed when I finally retired late that evening. She'd already fallen asleep, drooling into my pillow.

Anton invited nearly every unmarried woman in the city of Plav. He didn't understand my absolute refusal to consider anyone under the age of eighteen. So my ballroom was filled with the merry laughter of children and music.

Several girls made their pitch as to why their family would offer a better alliance than another; I just couldn't take them seriously. Overall, the children had fun amongst themselves. None of them danced, though a few tried to copy their chaperones by standing and talking. Most of them romped around the dance floor and had a good time.

Anton stood by my side as we looked over our guests. He let out a big sigh, "I apologize, your Grace."

I nodded to him, but didn't say anything.

"Several families didn't understand. I didn't understand," he hung his head. "I do now."

I clapped him on the shoulder and said, "Good. This won't happen again."

"It will not, your Grace," Anton bowed.

"Well, I don't understand," a light voice said from behind us.

Anton and I turned to face the speaker. She had honey light brown hair and eyes, and her charms on full display with how short she was.

"I've heard about your 'conditions' and I meet most of them, but I'm seventeen," she planted her fists on her hips. "What difference does a year make?"

I nodded, "Because, then the age of acceptance is always pushed back. There will always be some sort of circumstance that inevitably demands an exception." I put on a face of mock horror. "Then the next thing I know, I'm married to an infant."

She giggled then bowed, "I am the heir-apparent of Countess Devereaux, Emily Devereaux."

"I am pleased to make your acquaintance, Lady Emily," I gave her a half bow.

"So there is no hope for me, your Grace?" Emily pouted.

I was about to say no, when Anton cleared his throat. I gestured to him and he said, "Your Grace, would you be willing to consider a year long betrothal?"

I tiled my head back as I considered his words. He continued, "It doesn't have to be a formal betrothal. Just a period of time for you both to get to know one another."

"My mother would insist on a formal betrothal, Lord Kos," Emily looked at the ground forlorn. "She doesn't agree with, his Grace's, peculiarities."

I wasn't comfortable with the situation at best, but this wasn't about us as people. Any marriage I had would be based on political power and maneuvering. The individuals involved weren't seen as people, just commodities to be traded. That's why age didn't matter to these people. These children were pawns to help build on the legacies of their families.

But, could I afford to wait a year? I'd already sent overtures to a couple of merchant associations and they'd been leery of signing any multigenerational agreements due to my current marital status. They wanted the assurance that any long-term treatise would pass along to my children. If I wasn't even married? Not a chance. Many of my future plans for the people of Montenegro depended upon me marrying a noblewoman.

I nodded to Anton, "Begin a dialog with Lady Emily's

chaperone."

Anton smiled. Emily smiled. Her chaperone smiled. Why did I feel so slimy?

Anton and Emily's chaperone walked a few meters away to confer.

Emily looked at me and bounced her eyebrows up and down, "Whatever shall we do, Milord?"

"Not that," I said firmly. "I will not begrudge you your past, but from now, until the wedding, you will abstain from such activities."

Emily frowned at me, "I will do as you *ask*. Though I don't appreciate your judgment about me."

"I apologize," I said. "But, the magic of Mithira doesn't care about the current customs of Montenegro. Only my child will inherit the Duchy. So to prevent any future inheritance problems, there will only be children of my line, from my wife."

"I didn't know," Emily frowned in thought. "It does make sense, but the entire concept is alien to me. What did you mean by 'current customs?'"

"Before the Unification, the hereditary order followed the male line."

"Men were in charge?" She asked, shocked.

I saw a servant with a tray full of drinks and beckoned her over.

"What is your pleasure, your Grace?"

"The Raegon, please," I looked at Emily and smiling, she said, "White wine, any will do."

"I will be right back, your Grace," the servant said and quickly strode away.

Emily and I chatted amicably for a few minutes until the drinks arrived.

"What is that stench? Is it coming from your glass?" Emily made a retching face. "Oh, that won't do at all," she made to reach for the whiskey in my hand, and I gently lifted it beyond her reach.

Anton came over quickly, "What seems to be the problem, your Grace?"

"It appears that young Emily here is quite opinionated about my choice of libation. A true shame."

Anton closed his eyes and sighed. His slouched posture got Emily's attention.

"Wait, what is going on here?" Her voice steadily rose as she looked around, before settling her gaze on me. "Over a drink? Are you serious?"

The memory of Amanda settled over me like a cloud. "Quite serious. Enjoy the rest of your evening."

I went to turn away, but caught a face full of wine before I could make it all the way around. I cast my new cleanse spell as I turned back around.

"Do you feel better, little girl? Everything right in your world again?"

Her cheeks flushed as she glared daggers at me. "Why? Why end this over a drink?"

"Nothing to end, if it never began," I said. "I'm not one of the boys who chase after you. You don't get to tell me what to do."

"That's what this is about? Power? You want to lord over me like our barbaric ancestors used to?"

"Sure," I dismissed her and turned to leave. "Whatever helps you sleep at night."

I made it three steps before a thrown wine glass broke over my shield. It could have been worse, I honestly expected her to throw a fireball, or something more lethal than glassware.

"I'm not playing the same game here, that you are," I said, turning back to her. "You seek advancement for yourself and maybe your House. I play for higher stakes, in a grander game."

"Oh really," the amount of scorn in her voice was palpable. "Just what 'Grander' game do you play? My lord?"

"I work for the betterment, and enrichment, of all our people," I said simply.

"You are a fool," Emily said. "You have a duty to your gentry, to see them prosper. It is the responsibility of the nobles, to see to their commoners." She pointed at me. "You have no right to undercut the authority of the aristocracy that has been maintaining this land for generations."

"I, as Duke, have every right," I told her, my face bland. "The 'commoners' are people. And they are, all of them, my responsibility." I took the time to make eye contact with as many of the people watching this train wreck as possible, to include them as more than bystanders in a lover's spat.

"To think that generations have squandered their responsibilities, to simply enrich themselves to a moderate degree," I gestured expansively. "I traveled through some of Neves recently. They put you to shame, in wealth, and the treatment of the common people. How? Why?"

Emily scowled at me and crossed her arms, but didn't answer.

I glanced again at the growing crowd and addressed them all, "Because they know that a robust economy must have a strong base." I tilted my head from side-to-side, "Of course, they could do better, but why would I give our competition pointers?"

Emily shook her head, "It all sounds grand, this vague plan of yours." She raised her arms to shoulder height and palms facing the ceiling, "What happens when you face open rebellion from the aristocracy? You've already offended several Houses with your petty demands for courtship, and throwing innocent nobles on to the street after they legally bought property." She smirked, and asked snidely, "Tell me, Duke Montenegro, what will you do when powerful nobles reject you?"

"Execute them for treason, and raise up others more worthy to take their places."

It was my turn to smirk as her jaw fell open.

"What?" I asked. "If they do not give oath to me then the land, and titles, revert to me. If they break their oaths to me, then they are traitors, and will be dealt with accordingly."

"But, the Queen," Emily frowned in thought, and I overrode her.

"Does not guarantee the survival of your House, in the face of rebellion against your suzerain." I said loud enough to be heard across the wide room. "Let me be clear, I want cooperation, but I will not brook treason. It is a painful process raising commoners to the aristocracy," I made a face of mock horror. "It is hours upon hours of paperwork. That someone else would have to do," I finished archly.

The server who stood close by, the same woman from before, giggled softly before pressing her lips together firmly. But, Emily heard her, and she didn't share the sentiment.

"Get out! You're fired!" Emily's eyes blazed. "You will never work in this city again! I'll make sure of that!"

I looked at Anton, who rolled his eyes and made his way to intercept the server.

I saw that the woman raised her hand above her head then moved her arm in a circle three times. About two dozen men and women, either put their trays down on the floor, or appeared from the shadows of the room from where they waited to be of service. Hopefully, I'll have a full service staff shortly.

"Ah," I said laconically as Emily stalked away. "And the evening was going so well."

I nodded to Anton as he watched me leave the ballroom while he spoke with the woman who thought I was funny.

I sat and waited in the carriage for Anton to finish up the business that I threw in his lap. I was lucky to have him. I should probably tell him to give himself a raise. I chuckled to myself.

After a quick knock, the door opened and Anton entered the carriage, looked around, frowned then shook his head.

"Ms. Blount will come by tomorrow morning to negotiate the services of her business."

I raised an eyebrow as the carriage began moving. "Didn't Master Sin-Nasir already hire them?"

"Yes, well," Anton coughed gently. "She seems to have the opinion that this is all your fault."

My other eyebrow joined the first one in its race to my scalp.

"I told her your charm couldn't possibly be to blame, your Grace, for her miss timed mirth," Anton sat back and crossed his legs at the knee. "I do think that it is more that she wants to make sure that her people are well cared for. She was quite moved when you said, you have a responsibility for all your people."

I winced. I didn't mean a personal responsibility. More like, my position was responsible for their welfare, in general. I'm sure this wasn't going to bite me in the butt later on.

"Well, if they are going to uproot their families and move to the capital, then I see no problem with paying more," I looked at him seriously. "Even more so, if they are willing to take an oath. We will need others who can be trusted not to poison our food and drink."

Anton nodded and tugged at his tunic. I hadn't noticed it before, but it looked like a uniform. A little anyway. My House colors showed prominently with straight lines in the cut of the garment. Anton wore a gold Phoenix pinned to the high collar.

I met his eyes as my gaze drifted to his, and he blushed. I smiled and said, "I like it. Thank you."

"Of course, your Grace," he said as he looked down at his lap.

Chapter 19

I sorted through the different financial accounts I'd requested from innkeepers before my meeting with Ms. Blount. They all differed in multiple, separate ways, in which they charged their guests. I wanted to convince them to adopt a more uniform way to set a cost to service ratio. That way visiting merchants would have a better way to budget their expenses when traveling within Montenegro. More merchants meant more trade, which in turn increased the volume of coin staying in the

Duchy. It also increased the volume from which taxes were collected.

No one likes taxes, especially the people who pay them, even those who collect them don't like to pay them for the most part. A few deviants always fell through the cracks, but taxes are a necessary evil for all involved. Roads, commerce, and troops need money to keep moving. And I didn't have a standing army to meet a threat to the Duchy with. No, I was supposed to work with the aristocracy, so that they could call up their militia, and draft whatever peasants they thought necessary, for repelling various threats. Because I'm sure that would work out in my favor.

My own personal coffers would suffice, for now, to build up the infrastructure the Duchy so desperately needed. That wasn't sustainable long term. Those funds were supposed to build up my own holdings, and raise my people up out of poverty. I couldn't focus too much attention on any one area, because the aristocracy didn't do the work they were supposed to be doing.

"Your Grace, Ms. Blount is here to see you," Anton announced from the door.

I looked up from my paperwork in time to see Ms. Blount throw Anton a smile as she tucked a strand of light brown hair behind her ear. I motioned to a chair at the table adjacent to me.

"Please, have a seat Ms. Blount," I said.

She smoothed the front of her green, blue, and white dress before she made her way over. She seemed to shrink in on herself as she got closer to the chair. Her nervousness showed as she fidgeted with her hair and dress.

"Mr. Kos said you had some concerns, Ms. Blount?" I asked her to get the conversation going.

"Yes, my Lord. I mean, your Grace," she blushed then pulled at the hair over her shoulder.

I waved dismissively, "I'm not concerned with formality in private."

"Of course, your Grace," she placed her hands firmly in her lap and tried to smile. Her brown eyes would meet mine only in short bursts. I was pretty sure she was going to make herself dizzy in a minute.

I waited for her to begin the negotiations, but she remained quiet. I couldn't keep in my sigh of frustration.

"So, I am offering you a contract for your services. Will your people be coming with you? Will they bring their families with them?"

"Yes, your Grace."

"I see," I said. I didn't because she acted like I was going to pounce on her at any moment. Wait a minute.

"Let me try to put your mind at ease," I folded my hands on the table top. "I need a service staff that I can trust. I do not need bed warmers, or anything sexually related."

Her eyes widened and she thinned her lips. Maybe I had the wrong impression.

"Are you alright Ms. Blount?" I asked. "You seem unnecessarily distraught."

"No. I mean, I'm fine," she sputtered. "Your Grace. Oh bother." Ms. Blunt covered her face with her hands.

"We can speak another time, perhaps," I shuffled my paperwork around until I found what I wanted, and slid the contract over to her. "Look that over, Ms. Blount, and see if it is acceptable for you. Speak with Mr. Kos if you have any questions or concerns, then give him the signed contract if you accept our terms."

Ms. Blount took the paper with a hand that shook so much it rattled noisily. She practically fled my presence. Odd woman.

Anton stuck his head through the doorway, frowned, then hurried after the woman. I shrugged and continued working.

I jotted down some figures when a knock sounded from the

door. "Enter," I said.

Anton came in, followed by a portly man, and a woman who was only slightly thinner. Both had nondescript brown hair and eyes. There was nothing remarkable about either of their appearance. They almost seemed to blend into the background, and even with their bright clothing would blend right in with the crowds of the city.

"Your Grace, may I present Mrs. and Mr. Downing?," Anton said with a bow.

"Please, won't you come in," I said, then I gestured to the chairs on the opposite side of the table. Both bowed their acceptance and sat.

The meeting lasted through lunch, and was as boring as one would expect people going over financial figures would be. Thankfully the wife and husband didn't try to stab me from over the table. They seemed happy enough when they left, satisfied that they could get other innkeepers to join the guild and be certified by the Duchy as a quality establishment. There was a little hesitation on the star system I wanted to introduce, but they agreed readily enough.

One to five stars indicated the quality of service of the Inn in question from least to most. It also reflected the cost of one's stay per night. The minimum agreed on, to be certified, was three stars. This would encourage other innkeepers to hire more staff to qualify for my seal of approval. A larger workforce meant a larger tax base to pull from.

After that I set up the Risin Foundation to give any refugees, or others down-on-their-luck, a place to sleep, and work to earn coin. Anton saw to hiring managers for me that would oversee the job training and apprenticeship for those interested. We used some of my newly vacated properties to house those who qualified.

That evening we hosted a dinner for Lady Lancaster and a few guests. Sin-Nasir wowed the nobles with his culinary creations and wine pairings. The event went well, with the help of Ms. Blount and her people attending to the needs of my guests, in a professional manner. My goal to cement Lady Lancaster as an ally, without joining our Houses in marriage, took root when she expressed an interest in the Risin Foundation.

"And this idea is from Lord Risin, your Grace?" Lady Lancaster asked.

"Truly, my Lady, and the town of Risin is clean and orderly. A wonderful example of how the aristocracy can make a positive change in the lives of the people, and enrich themselves at the same time."

Several heads around the table nodded along.

"I would like to help, your Grace," she said. "Do you have any suggestions on how my House can gain notoriety in a similar manner?"

I sat back and scratched my beard while I thought for a moment. "You could set up a school for craftsmen and trades. Have a scholarship and loan program in place to help the poor get started earning their way."

I smiled at her, "You could call it the, 'Lancaster institute of technology,' lighting the way for prosperity."

"Oh, that sounds wonderful, your Grace," Annette gushed.

I nodded, accepting the compliment at face value.

"But, your Grace," a pasty-faced woman from further down the table drew attention to herself. "How does this investment into the commoners pay itself back?"

I looked at her squarely, "Let's say you have one in every one hundred commoners making a Crown a year. You make ten Marks from her in taxes." The noble woman nodded her understanding. "With these investments in training, you can have seventy-five people paying ten Marks each for taxes. Now you earn a Crown per one hundred. With more coin to spend, more commoners will have more children, and thereby increase your tax base."

She leaned forward and I smirked at her, "The trick, is in *how* you collect taxes." Many of the nobles around the table frowned. "Tax the merchants. The shopkeepers will pass on that cost to the buyer and won't be quite as likely to evade the tax. Especially if it is rather low and their goods are protected."

I brushed off the looks of awe. It wasn't like I came up with the idea myself. In one way or another, we all stand on the shoulders of giants to look for new horizons.

"This is a generational plan, my Ladies," I said looking down the table. "This won't make us all rich overnight, but over the next ten years we will see a significant increase in our wealth."

I leaned a little closer to Annette, but still addressed the room, "The Bank and Trust of Montenegro can issue loans based on projected tax revenues."

A cacophony of murmurs cascaded down the table.

"Your Grace," a handsome woman with uncommon blue eyes raised her hand. She continued as my gaze settled on her. "What would be the terms of such a loan?"

"Well," I smiled and said. "It would be on a case by case basis, but the more you ask for, the more you put up for collateral."

"What is acceptable as collateral, your Grace?" Another woman asked. She then sank down into her chair as others around the table looked at her.

"Land is the most commonly accepted," I tapped my lips with

one finger. "Some heirloom valuables might be acceptable. But, it would, like I said previously, be on a case by case basis."

Several heads nodded, and a few women raised their hands. I got them interested in the idea, now I needed them to come to the open house to ask their questions.

I held up both of my hands to gather their attention. When the table quieted down I said, "My Ladies, the Bank will open in one week. Please save your questions for then and you can have more specific answers, in private, at that time. I will ensure there are enough staff at the office to see to everyone in a timely manner."

I took on a thoughtful manner. "As a matter of fact," I paused for a moment. "I'll make sure there is a nobles only section for all the Lords and Ladies who might be interested."

I settled back in my seat as the women went back to speaking amongst themselves. Lady Lancaster frowned off into the distance. Sometimes one had to forge their own keys of power.

All in all, today was a success, if excessively long. I activated the magic runes for the shower, and the water was ready to use. I disrobed, got in the shower, and made the best of the time I had to myself.

I was almost finished drying my hair, when I heard a tap on my bedroom window. I walked out of the bathroom in time to see someone climb through the window and activate the ward.

I didn't specialize in wards. Nor did I have much experience with mentalism. So, my wards were still basic things that didn't differentiate on what someone's motivation might be. If someone crossed the ward, then it would activate according to the type that was spelled. A non-lethal type to secure the capture of an intruder in this case.

When the person made it halfway through the window, the electric shock of lightning knocked them unconscious. The ward did not take into account the dagger that person fell upon.

A few moments and more muttered curses later, the body pushed through the window to fall limply to the floor. I'd taken the time to walk to my desk, and open my coin purse, while the others struggled to move the body of their comrade.

Three people entered, then stared down at the dead body on the floor. The shock was apparent, even through their masks, to find a naked man gazing at them calmly.

"Why is he naked?," a feminine voice hissed.

"I don't know, but damn," a different female said aloud.

The third person turned to face the two women and asked,

"Really?"

I rolled my eyes and said, "If you drop your weapons, and lay down on the floor, you can live through this fiasco."

"Only if you lay down with me," one of the women said in a husky voice.

All three drew daggers and advanced two steps. That was as close as I let them get to me, before I teleported a coin into each of their skulls. The three thumped to the ground lifeless.

I grabbed a robe and threw it on, before I opened my bedroom door. "Guards!" I shouted. "I have intruders and they need to be removed."

Captain Jur stood over the unmasked women. I stood behind him as he looked for clues as to who my assailants were. "Your Grace, you may wish to leave," he grimaced. "They don't have anything in their pockets, so I will remove their clothes to see if they have any identifying marks."

I shook my head, "Carry on Captain Jur, it won't bother me."

They were women born like any others, having all the requisite parts where they should be. Something these women did have extra, was a crescent moon mark or tattoo, on the left breast, cupped around the areola.

The tips of the moon pointed toward the head of each woman

regardless of the different sizes in body shape. Other than the odd hairlessness that seemed to pervade the culture, there were no more identifying marks on the bodies.

"Any ideas Captain?" I asked.

"No, your Grace," Jur shook his head. "I'm not familiar with this mark. Though in all fairness, I'm only familiar with a couple of well known assassin marks." He looked around the room a bit more and shook his head again. "If I had to make a guess, I'd say that these three are initiates of an amateur gang. Why they thought attacking you would be a good idea is beyond me."

"I'm certain they were chosen for being amateurs," Lord Jellinek said.

I looked back at him where he stood in the doorway, "What makes you say that?"

"An insult is given either way. They show what they think of you, even if the assassination attempt fails," his lip curled in a sneer. "A contemptible waste of life."

"So you think this is a message?"

"Yes, your Grace."

"What do you think, Captain Jur?"

"I am inclined," he nodded to Lord Jellinek. "To agree with

Lord Jellinek. Though, I will say I'm not certain about anything at all."

"I will take the guest room for the night," I said. "Please, have a couple guards below the window." I frowned in thought. Could this be a decoy attack? "On second thought, have a pair of guards in the room below mine, keeping an eye on the window directly below mine. Then have a roving pair move around the manor."

"Aye, your Grace. Two hour shifts?" Captain Jur asked.

"That's a good idea. I'm off to get some sleep. Goodnight gentlemen."

"Good night, your Grace," they said at the same time. It had to be something they practiced.

Chapter 20

Fifteen days in Plav. With the exception of my winter, staying in the wagon when I first arrived, this was my longest stay anywhere in Tallinn. Hopefully it wouldn't last more than a few more days at the most.

The merchants who had traveled with us before had left already. They would no doubt spread the news of a new Duke of Montenegro. I had to stay to see the Bank open, which was scheduled for tomorrow. Without the heavy merchant wagons, we should enter the capital in a week. I looked forward to seeing my new home for the first time. When I'd previously asked about what the capital looked like, Anton said he didn't want to ruin the surprise. I suspected he'd never been there.

I performed my morning routine like normal. Though, I was glad that Edward was able to find me some lotions for my beard. The itching just about drove me crazy. Maybe that was why I'd been so short tempered lately. I dressed and made my way down to breakfast.

After I ate, Anton handed me a large number of envelopes. Most of them were invitations to one party/gathering or another that I possessed no interest in attending. Several of the letters were good news. The Cardinal of Mithira would be honored and pleased, to perform the coronation himself. The Welkin Palace reported complete readiness for their Duke to take residence. The curator, Mr. Lambert, went on to say that all museum pieces have been replaced with accurate, usable replicas. A full accounting is available to verify that all antiques are in storage, and not in unsavory hands. In all honesty, it never crossed my mind before now. But, good news is good news.

After reading my correspondence, I notified Anton that I'd be in the study. I'd use my leisure time to learn more about spell craft and theory. I worked on my Arcane Bolt spell. I really wanted it to follow whomever I targeted. Unfortunately, the target rune did not want to play well with other runes. The mildest reaction I could expect was explosive. Not something I wanted to experience a couple of feet from my face. But, I could place a spell, better known as a Hex, that would make the target easier to hit with a follow up spell. I went ahead and learned the Hex. Because better to have it and not need it, than need it and not have it.

I also looked into enchantments. They fascinated me and were the height of technology here in Tallinn. The practice of enchanting needed to be completed, from start to finish, by the Wizard who was making the piece. They needed to imbue their mana almost constantly at every step of the way. The engraving of each rune differed in every dimension and amount of mana needed while crafted. It was very labor intensive, and the knowledge base needed for even the simplest of gadgets was immense.

I had a new appreciation for my shower, after learning about how it was created. I just didn't have the time to dedicate myself to learning the practice. And as cool as I thought these objects were, I didn't have the passion to sit for hours on end, to learn about how to craft them. Or, to sit and actually carve out each and every rune, and connecting glyphs, of the different parts and pieces that make up even the simplest of devices.

So, I went back to learning the runic language of spells. And I know how that sounds, why not use one for the other? Because enchantments use a different language, specific to physical objects. Oftentimes, the runes will mean different things when used on different materials. Someone who enchants arms and armor, wouldn't have the correct runes to enchant clothing, or showers, and vice versa.

The other difference was that I could compact my spell structures in a three dimensional space, without considering layers of intervening material. My spell, Light ball, only needed a simple spell circle. Scorching Detonation needed twenty-seven different diameter circles that when connected by the appropriate glyphs, made a compact sphere. Its size was only limited by my mana, and my compression of the spell. If I could visualize it to the size of a pea, then I would consider that spell mastered. Without a teacher, I really couldn't objectively judge my skill level with any accuracy.

After a long day with my head in my books, I retired from the study. Anton met me in the dining room.

"Everything is well, Mr. Kos?" I asked.

Anton nodded and said, "It is, your Grace." He placed his napkin on his lap. "The Bank of Montenegro in Plav will open on time tomorrow."

I nodded and said, "Excellent. Please make sure we will have everything we need for the trip to the capital." I paused for a moment. "I'd hate to leave people behind, but I cannot be late."

"I will see to it personally, your Grace," Anton bowed in his seat.

We had a soup that reminded me of minestrone with breadsticks. The whole meal had an Italian feel and flavor, from the light salad to the clam, shrimp, and scallop pasta. For dessert Sin-Nasir made a wonderful crème brûlée.

I slept in my own bed that night. No trace of the assassination attempt remained, in the room or my head.

The cool morning air pushed my beard to the side, as I stood there with scissors, to cut a ribbon for about twenty nobles and ten times that number of commoners. The security of having a place where your hard earned money would be safe drew people in, and nothing draws a crowd like a crowd. Soon, the square in front of the bank was packed with people.

I didn't give a big rousing speech. I did not take the time to make this a political event. It wasn't like I was an elected official. The people were stuck with me for the rest of my life. I gave some brief information about the bank, they could ask questions inside, then I cut the ribbon. I gave a half bow to the nobles then left.

"That went well," I said to Anton as we rode in the carriage to the southern gate to leave the city.

"It did, your Grace," Anton nodded. "As will your coronation."

"Am I that easy to read?" I asked.

"To me you are," Anton smiled serenely. "But, anyone would be nervous in your situation, even someone born knowing that they would, one day stand in front of thousands of people. All of them judging, and weighing you, wondering about your worthiness to lead."

"Yeah," I sank down and tried to hide in the cushions. "Thanks."

"Of course, your Grace," Anton still wore his benevolent smile. "Anytime."

"Are you still mad about Lady Bouvier?" I asked.

"Of course not, your Grace," Anton said with a twinkle in his eye. "I'm sure she was a handsome woman in her time." He crossed his legs and placed his hands on top, "Even though that time was fifty years ago, I'm sure she would have made me a wonderful wife."

"I'm sorry," I said. And I meant it. "It was supposed to be a joke. I didn't think she would take it seriously. Hell, she proposed to me first." I shook my head. "I certainly didn't expect her to accept my counter proposal for you."

"But not when she promptly dropped dead of heart failure? How about just before she declared me her husband in front of witnesses?"

"Okay, no one was really shocked at that first one," I shrugged. "Everyone around her looked like perched vultures waiting for her final breath."

"What about her decision to instantly wed?" Anton asked pointedly.

"Look, I said I was sorry, Lord Anton Kos Bouvier," he threw a pillow at me. I picked it up and held it in front of me like a shield. "In my defense, I didn't even think it would stick. Who knew that her family was in such desperate need of a connection to the Duke?"

I blocked one pillow to the head, the second one hit me in the stomach.

"Look at the bright side," I dodged another pillow aimed at my head. "Your marital duties are done," another dodge. "Your wife had half a dozen children, and scores of grandchildren," blocked another. I didn't know we had so many pillows in here. "Now you can sit back and let the younger generation raise your House to power, oof." I missed that one.

A knock sounded from the carriage door before it opened and Captain Jur asked, "Is everything okay in here, Lord Bouvier?" Jur took a pillow to the face.

Poor Dazz was holding his sides while tears streamed down his face. He was so out of breath that no sound emerged from his laughter.

Anton sighed miserably then proceeded to ignore us for the rest of the day.

The old lady knew how to set an ambush, I'll give her that. Almost as soon as we reached the carriage from across the square, Lady Bouvier and her entourage stepped into our path, and asked me in her quivering voice, "You need to get married, and I'm looking for another husband, what do you say?"

I blinked rapidly for a moment, "Alas, my Lady, I cannot." Her left eye began to droop. "But, my Chancellor here is available."

"Done," her eyes brightened a moment. "Dongle, recognize for the record, that," she flopped her hand around, vaguely in Anton's direction. "Man, is now my husband." She then collapsed to the ground as if all her strings were cut at once.

Poor Anton looked on, gaping like a fish out of water.

Dongle stepped up to Anton and said, "My Lord, if you will sign here." He flipped the page, "And here."

Anton, in his shock, didn't take his eyes off the old woman as her kin carried her away, and signed the indicated pages.

"This last one here, Milord," Dongle took the signed paper, rolled them up, and tied them with a ribbon. He handed the scroll to Anton. "Excellent. Thank you, Lord Bouvier, may you serve your House proudly, and with honor."

Anton shook himself from his stupor a moment too late. "Who are you? What is this?"

"Donald Bouvier, my Lord, third cousin on my father's side. And that is your marriage certificate, peerage registration, and your acceptance of your late wife's appointment for you to be her executor."

Anton looked at me aghast, "Your Grace?"

I was stumped. My every experience with the nobility said that they wouldn't raise a commoner willingly and not this quickly. I looked at Dongle. I mean Donald, who quickly said, "The documents are legitimate, and the magical transcript copies are filed by now.

I looked back to Anton and shrugged, "Congratulations?"

Anton looked back and forth between Dongle and myself.

I turned back and said, "Look, Dongle."

"Donald," he corrected me.

"Whatever, did you just ambush my Chancellor into your family?"

"I assure you, your Grace," Dongle said with aplomb. "That you were the original target." He shook his head, "Sometimes Great-great-grandmother just took the reins, and put us on a different path. This is no different to us."

"Yeah, I get that," I thumbed back to Anton. "But he, I'm pretty sure, does not."

"I understand, your Grace, I truly do," Dongle spread his hands. "But, it is done."

I frowned, "I haven't ratified the appointment to the peerage."

"Duke Osvaldo gave our family a writ, for aiding his family, during his troubles," Dongle folded his hands, the very picture of solemn sacrifice. "That writ is still legal today, and with Lord Bouvier's signature, he is now family."

"But," Anton sounded pained. "I can't."

"My Lord," Dongle began.

"Can't," Anton looked angry now. "Because I am menos."

Dongle took a step back and looked between Anton and I.

"Not him, Dongle."

"Donald."

"Me," Anton continued as if he wasn't interrupted. "The law clearly states—"

"That an heir and a pair must be provided for," Dongle interrupted again.

Anton looked at me and said, "You can fix this."

"My friend, I will look into this," I told him seriously. "I'm sure there is a provision for coercion or fraud."

I stopped as Dongle shook his head.

"Why would there be in this case?" Dongle asked exasperated. "Who would seek to avoid such an honor?"

"But?" Anton stopped when Dongle shook his head, and walked away. Lord Anton Bouvier looked at me wide-eyed. I shrugged helplessly.

Chapter 21

Anton still wasn't talking to me the next day. Dazz looked on, with worry creasing his brow, as Anton sunk into himself. I'd give him another day to get his shit together. Like Dongle said, no one in their right mind turns down entrance into the aristocracy.

So I spent my time cultivating my Core. I formed, folded, and compressed my mana. I meditated. I worried for the future. I planned some of my political moves in advance. I worked with my mana some more. I settled deep inside myself, and pushed the folded mana into my Core. It was much easier to work with compared to before. The task itself was difficult, but working with unrefined mana to increase my Core, was like trying to force oil back into a hydraulic press. With my bare hands. Now, it was like pushing bread dough into a too small pan. Eventually, my grumbling stomach pains brought me back to awareness.

"Your Grace!" Anton shouted. "Are you alright?"

I blinked rapidly and focused on him. "Yeah, I'm fine."

"Good," his face was pinched and scrunched up. "But, Mother Mithira have Mercy, what is that stench?"

"What?" I lifted the back of my hand to my nose and recoiled. "Ugh!"

"I know, Milord, it started an hour ago," Anton glared through his disgust.

"Let's stop the caravan, and I'll get cleaned up," I shrugged when Anton lifted his hands and wiggled his fingers. "The stuff still has to go somewhere, and I figure that shouldn't be here."

"Quite right, your Grace," Lord Anton Bouvier still glared at me. "What an amazing amount of foresight you've developed in such a short amount of time."

"Thank you," I knuckled my forehead. "Milord."

"Ugh," Anton grunted. "I can taste it," he gagged. "Ah thing ahts ah mah thung." He began to wretch.

I threw open the door and hung Anton out the carriage. The enchantments kept his sick from sticking to the side.

A trooper galloped over and asked, "Is everything? Oh!" His eyes went wide, but his face tried to pinch closed, to flee from the smell.

"Get everyone stopped!" I shouted.

He nodded with such vigor that I worried for a moment that he'd hurt himself, he spurred his horse, and rode away quickly.

Soon after, I was naked, and alone in a clump of bushes, casting my Cleanse spell for the fourth time. My carriage sat isolated on a little rise, so the sea breeze could air it out some. After I'd used a quarter of my mana, which is a ridiculous amount, considering that the spell normally doesn't make an impact on my mana pool, my clothes and I were finally clean.

My Aura of Ambiance was going full blast as I neared the carriage. Fully clothed, I got closer, but didn't smell anything. It wasn't until I got to the door that I noticed any smell at all. Gray goop looked like it had oozed from the traveling compartment, and plopped down into the grass. I let go of the power that I pumped into the aura. There was a faint scent in the air, though nothing I thought we couldn't manage.

I stuck my head inside, and looked at where I normally sat. There was nothing there. Just as pristine as always. The enchantments repelled the toxic sludge I expelled with my cultivation. I needed to remember that for the future. To not cultivate in a cramped space in front of other people. That ended up an embarrassing moment that I'm sure Anton will forget about soon.

An uneventful three days passed before we caught sight of the capital. Though filled with little cutting comments from Anton, he never crossed the line, and we all laughed as he ribbed me. We were still two days away from entering the gates, but the black mountain that loomed over the capital, pierced the sky in the distance. Lord Jellinek swore he could see the flags of the Palace flash in the distance.

That night I stood on a bluff over the sea. The breeze carried a salty tang that reminded me of how I proposed to Amanda on the beach. I smiled through the bittersweet memory. While I missed the small amenities that my world offered, air conditioning and fast food placing at the top of the list, I didn't miss her. No, I wouldn't go back. Ever. This world offered things that normally only existed in dreams. The Prince in my very own fairy tale. I'll acknowledge that I'm not charming, but rich people have manners all their own.

In an effort to save time, and avoid unnecessary entanglements, we passed by the small villages and hamlets on the way to the capital. I needed to give the capital a name, most cities grew up with a name, though for some reason they skipped that step with the capital. I'm pretty sure they called it Montenegro somewhere in the past, though no one I traveled with knew much of the history of the Duchy.

The polished gleam of the black walls of Montenegro shone in the morning sun. My personal entourage escorted us to the gates, while Lord Jellinek and his men protected the families a day behind us. Sin-Nasir, Mr. Silva, and my newly hired staff rode in four wagons behind my carriage, as Captain Jur ensured our security. Anton sighed audibly when I nearly stuck my head out the window, and gaped like a tourist. The guards at the open gate took one look at the carriage and waved us through. I don't think they knew who we were, just that we must be someone important, and didn't want that kind of involvement. I empathized with them.

The streets, while narrow, allowed different vehicles to pass both ways. The extra wide sidewalks however, carried the press of humanity on either side. Men scooped and shoveled droppings like their lives depended upon it. Clean and orderly, was the first impression of my new home. I didn't see any refugees or the homeless sitting around. Filth didn't stain the buildings, and the detritus of humanity, in general, was lacking. But, this being a port city, I didn't get my hopes up too much. What goes out on the morning tide, comes back with the evening.

I wondered for a moment how our driver knew where to go, though when I pulled my gaze from the people, the Palace loomed in front of us up the street. And when I say up, I mean up. Mid-way up the side of the black jagged rock of the mountain, sat the Palace of Wilkin. Red and yellow flags flapped in the sea air, atop whimsical towers and flowing rooftops, carved from, and into the mountain. The Palace was magically majestic, and a little bit intimidating. That was supposed to be my home? The Monstrosity was an hour away at best. I had the, quite reasonable, fear of getting lost trying to find the bathroom.

At the base of the mountain, Captain Jur sent two men ahead up the switchbacks, to ready the way for our arrival. No need to surprise and fight my own guards on the way home. The heaviness of the word pressed down on me. Home. More than just a place to lay my head. I belonged to a larger community. Took responsibility for my impact on those around me. I was named Duke, and even acted the part, now this gigantic Palace brought crashing home the reality of my situation.

The guards greeted me with a salute, left fist to heart, and presented their spears at a precise forty-five degree angle.

The display smacked of pomp-and-circumstance, so I paid the men and women the honor of returning their salute. I knew I'd done the right thing when a young man cracked a smile, and looked mortified when Jur cleared his throat.

The front doors of the Palace dominated the view of the courtyard. White wood, banded with a matte black metal that soaked in the light around them, stood stark sentinel over the small humans waiting at attention. The teutonic woman who headed the group stood head and shoulders above the uniformly dressed, in red with yellow accented tunics, men and women that surrounded her. Her broad chest expanded as she drew in a deep breath before she bowed, followed a beat later by the large crowd.

The large woman's soft voice carried, unnaturally, to us as she straightened, "Your Grace, welcome home."

I gave her a half bow and said, "Thank you. It's been a long road." I smiled and met as many eyes as I could, "Thank you all for the extraordinary service in readying the Palace for my arrival. I am proud to call Wilkin Palace home."

I noticed a few small smiles here and there in the crowd, but most emulated their spokeswoman with stoic expressions.

"Let me introduce my companions," I gestured to the right of my group. "The captain of my protection detail, Jur Koval," Jur stood gobsmacked, staring in awe at the woman.

"My personal chef, Master Sin-Nasir," who bowed as if to an equal.

Back over to my left, "Here, we have Drazan Lenart, Healer and my Apprentice." Dazz bowed appropriately.

"My tailor, the renowned, Mr. Silva," Silva made a show of bowing with unnecessary flourishes.

"And last, but never least," I grasped Anton's shoulder. "Lord Anton Kos Bouvier, my Chancellor, chaperone, and Voice."

Anton frowned at my breaking protocol, but he bowed, then stepped forward. "An honor to meet you Madame," Anton turned to face me and bowed low to me then announced, "May I present his Grace, Duke Daniel Hawthorne del Montenegro, Prince of the realm, Lord Mage, and Head of House Montenegro."

The crowd bowed again, much lower this time.

"Your Grace, I am Lady Sara Cole," Sara said. "Seneschal of Wilkin Palace," her brow twitched at the worshipful gaze Jur continued to level at her. "Please, your Grace, don't let us keep you." Lady Sara clapped her hands twice, and the rest of the staff rushed to unload the carriage and wagons.

Sara turned to address a question, and I took that opportunity to elbow Jur in the ribs.

"Omph!" Jur, caught off guard, folded over, but straightened quickly when Sara looked over.

She gave us a soft smile and went back to directing her staff.

"What is with you?" I asked Jur.

"Your Grace, I'm sorry," he shrugged sheepishly. "I don't know what happened."

"It's fine," I said. "So long as you keep it together. Don't embarrass yourself." I clapped him on the shoulder and walked to Lady Sara.

"Lady Seneschal, would you be so kind as to show me around," I gestured toward the Palace. "I'm afraid I'd get hopelessly lost."

"It would be my honor, your Grace," she said. Her red skirt swirled as she turned and made her way to the massive white doors which started to open as we reached the first step.

The grand foyer we entered ran almost the full length of the front of the Palace. Narrow windows were spaced along the front wall, but the mirrors were masterfully placed to reflect the little light that made it through, to illuminate the entire room. Under the heavy mirrors, sat hardwood tables with flower filled vases. Tapestries hung throughout the rectangular foyer, softening the hard stone of the building.

We continued on and passed sitting rooms, a ballroom, a parlor, and I took special note of the restroom on the main corridor. We entered a large room, maybe thirty meters square, that held four staircases. We entered the north side of the Palace, and the stairs faced each of the cardinal directions, though the north side stairs were offset to our right by ten meters.

Lady Sara led me onto the south stairs into the mountain proper. The air cooled considerably a few meters into the solid rock. Before, we took a straight shot to the stairs, but now we traversed and crisscrossed a dozen different corridors in a weaving path that meandered to a luxurious set of rooms.

The family rooms of the Duke took up the east wing of the Palace. Most were empty, though the bright colors of the children's furniture held a hint of laughter. A chill ran down my spine when I remembered that someone murdered these kids. The people responsible were long dead, and logically, I couldn't hold their descendants accountable. The sins of the father didn't pass to the children.

Lady Sara stood by the door of the master suite as I looked around my new home. Fine furnishings decorated the various connected rooms. Bedroom, study, studio, bathroom, which contained the modern magical equivalent amenities I knew, and a sitting room belonged to me.

The future Duchess would have her own suite. The children would also have a suite of their own with connected spaces for nannies and wet nurses. The whole space felt like an ancient Roman villa that happened to be inside a mountain.

I sat down in a heavily cushioned, high backed chair, in the appropriate room for the deed, and held a child's ball in my hands. I'm not sure how long I sat, lost in my own thoughts; a gentle thump reminded me I wasn't alone, and I looked up.

"Are you well, your Grace?" Sara asked.

I met her eyes and said, "This will not happen again."

Her eyes searched mine briefly. I didn't know what she was looking for, or if she even found it, but she nodded slowly and said, "I believe you."

"Thank you," I tossed the ball up and caught it mentally. I set it to float off my right shoulder. "Did you have anything else to show me?"

Lady Sara nodded, "Yes, your Grace, but not immediately." She looked down at the floor and wet her lips.

"What's on your mind, Lady Sara?" I asked. When she still hesitated I said, "If we are going to work together, you need to be able to speak your mind." I gestured to the room around us, "When it is not in public, please, speak freely without fear."

She smirked at me, "You might come to regret that." She sat across from me and crossed her ankles.

I grinned back at her, "I'm sure I will." I chuckled at the shocked look on her face. "Please, continue, my Lady."

She fidgeted with her hands for a moment then said, "We are broke, your Grace." She spoke faster as she continued. "With the renovations and hiring new staff and cleaning and feeding everyone we…"

Sara trailed off as I pulled a wad of bank notes from a pocket in my robes and marked them.

I started with one thousand Crown notes, placing them down on the tea table in front of me. When I reached ten thousand Crowns I put down two, one hundred thousand Crown notes, that shocked Lady Sara from her stupor. She waved her hands at me to stop.

"Great Goddess, where did you come by so much coin?" She goggled, her eyes almost ready to pop. "Did you rob a bank?"

I smirked when I remembered the negotiations with the Royal Bank. "Not quite. But, I do own a few."

Her jaw dropped open, and her unblinking stare went on for several uncomfortable moments, before she shook herself.

"Your Grace, this is too much," her thick fingers daintily

touched the magically marked bank notes.

"Sweet Goddess, it is way too much," she whispered.

I waved her comment away, "I dare say it's not."

Her eyes widened.

"You are responsible for Palace upkeep, yes?" I asked.

"Yes, your Grace, but," she stopped at my upraised hand.

"If you don't have a ledger already, get one, and enter this as a deposit," I leaned forward. "Open an account with the Bank of Montenegro, and use it to pay our staff and guards, pay for repairs, and anything else necessary for the Palace. Your pay should also come out of the account as well." I scratched my beard in thought for a moment, "Oh, and see to my retinue as well."

Her deer in headlights look made me smile.

"Sin-Nasir, will prepare my meals, so he'll need his own space and supplies. Mr. Silva will need his own space and supplies as well, for the work he does," I tapped my lips with one finger. "You should get together with everyone to see what their specific needs are. Captain Jur will be especially pleased to speak to you."

A faint splotchy blush marred her cheeks, and she pushed her thin lips together in a firm line. "I will speak to him about appropriate," she seemed at a loss for words for a moment. "Things." Her blush deepened.

"Of course, my Lady," I nodded seriously.

"Very well, your Grace," Sara stood and bowed. "A very great many people will wish to see you. As per the instructions in your letter, Court has been called for this afternoon."

"Very well. Thank you Lady Sara. If you could have someone lead me to the appropriate place when the time comes?"

"Of course, your Grace, I will see to it."

"Excellent," I said as I walked her out of my suit.

Keep your friends close and your enemies closer, I thought to myself. *Cowards die many deaths before they meet their end. The valiant are slain only the once.*

Sun Tzu and Shakespeare, what more do you need when going to war?

Chapter 22

Lady Sara, when showing me around, didn't point out the narrow servant passageways. But I noticed them. So when the pressure of my responsibilities finally caught up to me, I used them to sneak out of the Palace. I'd changed out of my more formal garb, and dressed in my old clothes from Osvaldo.

I wasn't running away though. Too many people depended on me for that. People I could help, and make a difference in their lives. I felt the overwhelming urge to be me this one time. To be Daniel Hawthorne one last time. Not the Duke of Montenegro. Not, your Grace. Damn it all, it was like I didn't have a name anymore. Intellectually, I understood that I was more of a symbol than a man, to most of the people around me. Probably even to those closest to me. I just needed to set that hat down, let my hair out, and be myself. To be free one last time.

Which is how I found my way into a tavern near the docks, sipped warm beer, and laughed along with the other patrons at the ribald song one of the serving girls sang on top of a table. Her skirts lifted and fell as she kicked her feet while she danced. Her eyes gleamed as she looked down at me when the song ended, to the rousing cheers of the crowd. She extended a hand to me, to help her down, and her dimples flashed when she smiled.

She extended her hand out, palm up, "You, sir, owe me a Crown."

"That I do," I reached into my pocket and pulled one out, placing it gently into her hand. I thought I felt a spark as our skin touched.

She was a little breathless as she hooked her elbow to mine, and led me to a corner booth.

"So do you have any other ways for me to take your coin?" She asked.

I raised one eyebrow as I looked at her archly. She playfully slapped my arm, "Not that, you uncouth barbarian!" She lifted her head and sniffed, "I'm not that kind of girl." Then she broke into a fit of giggles.

"I would never dream of sullying your reputation, my Lady," I said in a lofty manner then gave my best impression of Mr. Silva's bow.

Her high tinkling laughter brought a grin to my face. She hooked her long dark hair behind her ears after wiping the laugh-tears from her eyes.

We sat down at the table, ordered more beer, and traded dirty jokes while we waited. A man stood in the doorway for an inordinate amount of time. Lieutenant Radlovic looked around and left. No sooner than I thought he might have missed me, he and two other troopers entered the establishment. A male server placed our beer mugs down on the table.

"That'll be four pennies." He scooped up the stack of coins I placed before him with practiced motion.

"Anything else I can get for you? How 'bout you, Tatiana? Fancy having a meal?"

Tatiana looked at me questioningly, and I motioned the question back to her. She just shrugged, so I looked at the man standing there hoping we'd order something else.

"I don't have time for a meal," I said as I saw Radlovic sit at a table close by. "What kind of snacks do you have?"

"What do you mean?"

"Something small and quick to make, usually salty so people order more drinks," he looked so dumbfounded that I took pity on him. "Any salted nuts? Chips?" He shook his head. "Toasted flatbread with cheese?"

He pointed at me excitedly, "That one I can do!" He looked around then leaned closer, "Salted nuts? Really?"

I nodded, "Usually you'd just put them out for people to munch on, then they'd get thirsty and order another drink." His shocked look made me explain. "No, you're not scamming your customers. They don't have to eat them and it's usually never so much to cause them problems. Just something to offer them so they want to spend more money."

He rapped the table with his knuckles then pointed at me, "This one's a keeper, Tia." Then he walked off muttering about nuts.

Tatiana blushed prettily and looked at me through her long lashes. Oh I'd sweep her off her feet if I could. She looked down at our drinks and placed a finger against her mug. It slowly frosted over. I looked at her sharply as hope swelled in my chest.

She turned bashful at my look and said, "It's just a trick. I'm not like those nobles with all their learning."

And just like that, my bubble of hope burst. My dejected sigh was a little too obvious.

"What? It's not that big of a deal."

"No, it is," I smiled. "As a matter of fact, did you know that the new Duke took up residence at the Palace?"

"No! What have you heard?" Tia placed her elbows on the table and leaned forward and loud-whispered, "I heard that his thing is only this big." She raised her hand up with her thumb and forefinger about three inches apart.

"What!?" I almost shouted appalled that such rumors about me were out there. "Where did you hear that?"

She grinned and bopped me on the nose, "You first." Her eyebrows bounced up and down.

I held in a sigh with effort. "Well, I know that the Duke will issue a call for all unaffiliated magic-users, no matter their advancement, to study and learn at the new school he's opening up."

"Great Goddess, really," she covered her mouth and her eyes shone with unshed tears. "I can learn?"

I nodded and smiled gently.

"Wait," she narrowed her eyes at me. "This isn't to pay me back for the 'little' joke, is it?"

Radlovic laughed, but when Tia and I both looked over, he was pointing to something across the room.

"No," I leaned forward like I had a secret and Tia matched my posture. "I met his Chancellor, Anton, at the scriveners' where he said that to the scribes."

I made a mental note to tell Anton to do just that. Though I was heartened to see the man to Radlovic's left writing furiously.

"This will be a dream come true," Tia said, tearing up again.

"I know what you mean," I said.

She started to say something, then stopped when I held my hand above my mug, and frost formed on it as I drew the heat out of it. I sent the energy to join the rest of the hot air in the tavern, on the ceiling.

"Oh," she blinked rapidly. "Will I see you there?"

"Absolutely," I grinned. I wondered how she'd react to seeing me after her 'little' joke.

The flat bread arrived and we chatted and drank beer. I had a wonderful time with her. I wished things were different, and if wishes were wings, frogs wouldn't bump their butts on lily pads. She's a special woman.

I saw Anton in the doorway looking frantic.

"My dear," I took her hand in mine. "You've been delightful. I'm glad I met you."

"That's it? You're leaving?" Her bottom lip stuck out in the cutest little pout.

"Alas, dearest, but I do have a prior engagement that simply won't wait on romance."

She blushed, and said, "You talk funny." Tia fiddled with her hair and asked, "Will you come back and see me?"

I grabbed her hand as she let it fall to her side, and lifted her hand to my lips. "If the Fates are kind, you will see me again."

Tia bit her bottom lip as she gazed at me with dark eyes, "I hope so."

I smiled, then turned and clapped Radlovic on the shoulder as I passed him on my way to the front door.

Anton sagged in relief. He looked ready to say something so I put a shushing finger to my lips. He frowned, but didn't say anything.

In the doorway, I turned back to see Tatiana and the barmaid giggling delightedly. She waved when she saw me looking and I waved back.

Anton cleared his throat and looked at me askance as we walked to the carriage parked beside the tavern.

"She's gifted, untrained, but gifted nonetheless," I said. Anton stayed silent. "I could see her as my wife, Anton."

"She is a commoner, your Grace," Anton said as we sat and he closed the door.

"She is anything, but common. She is an extraordinary woman. But," I held up a hand to forestall him. "She is of common birth. And unless my nobles give me cause, I cannot marry her."

We rode in silence for a time. I wasn't Daniel anymore. As soon as Anton spoke I turned back into, 'his Grace'. The beacon of hope for my people. The light of Grace for the aristocracy. Just, not a person. So be it. Everything comes with a price.

Chapter 23

"The poor girl sent to your rooms, to fetch you, panicked," Anton said, breaking the silence.

I chuckled, "I'm sure that was a sight."

Anton sighed, "What happened, Milord?"

I faced him directly. I could've prevaricated and deflected, I chose not to. I explained my thought process, and why I didn't take an escort with me.

"In the end it did me good to see the people, to feel the crowd, and remind myself why some difficult decisions are worth the effort."

"What do you mean, Milord?"

"That in the long run, it would be easier to just let the aristocracy do as they have been. If I just go with the flow, then I can sit back, relax, maybe take up hunting or some other nobles only sport," I turned and glowered out the window. "I could leave all the decisions to a wife, and study magic in peace."

Anton sat quietly, his hands folded in his lap.

"Until goblins overrun a starved land. Until the Binsar annex huge swaths of land, displacing even more people. It's not like the monarch is doing anything. I've not seen their presence once, in our travels," I rolled my eyes. "So long as they get their taxes they're fine."

I turned back to face him, "So, yeah. I needed to get this out of my system. And I won't promise not to do it again." I smirked at him. "It'll keep you on your toes."

Anton gave a polite chuckle, "I am sure it will, your Grace."

"So, I'll change when we get back, then meet the different House representatives."

Anton nodded, "Yes your Grace."

Thinking about it, I probably lost some of Anton's trust when I pulled my disappearing act. I could accept that. I didn't like it, but actions have consequences, and the little time away was worth it in the end.

A little over an hour later, dressed in my black robes trimmed in silver, I entered my, honest to god, humongous throne room. The throne itself stood proudly alone atop a dais at the back of the room. The monstrosity of a chair, wreathed in gilded wooden leaves, looked uncomfortable despite the royal purple cushions in the seat and armrests. Royal purple drapes, trimmed in silver with black scrollwork, hung in arches from the walls and around the only visible entrance to the room.

My entourage and I were the only people in the throne room. Our guests were finishing up their tour of the Palace.

I pointed up the wall, directly behind the throne, "I want a portrait of Osvaldo there."

"Your Grace?" Lady Sara asked as though I'd lost my mind. And to her thinking maybe I had.

"I want people to remember, where poor choices can lead them," I looked her in the eye. She looked away. Crazy and dangerous.

"Lady Cole," I said. "You will stand here to my left."

Anton smiled smugly.

"Lord Kos," his smile soured as I pointed. "you will stand to my right."

"Your Grace," Sara asked. "Is all this really necessary?"

Anton answered for me, "Yes, it is. These women will try to walk all over him if he doesn't shock them with this display." He shook his head. "It will save lives in the end."

I clapped my hands, "Too right." I pointed to Captain Jur. "Two men stationed behind the throne," I shook my head before he could protest. "No, we already talked about this. I am in no danger here. Your men on the other hand are. They stay along the walls so they can counter anything that might happen."

Jur sighed looking like a kicked puppy.

"That doesn't work on me, Captain," I heard surreptitious murmurs from the corridor. "Places everyone!"

The guards moved with celerity, while the Lord and Lady walked with sedate confidence to their assigned spots.

Women soon flowed through the entryway. Their looks were as varied as their mode of dress. Short and tall, fat and skinny, dark and light hair, though a few had darker complexions, most had fair skin. Tunics and pants were interspersed with dresses and gowns, with a few in skirts and blouses mixed in.

I sat and watched, as more than four hundred people entered, and grouped up in small crowds. Many seemed to jockey for positions near the front of the dais. I couldn't quite decide on how I should act at first. Should I be serious and scowl at everyone, or show a more lackadaisical, bored mien? I went with authenticity and slouched on the throne, elbow on the armrest while cupping my chin in my hand. I leaned to my right, towards Anton.

"Do you think they are wasting my time on purpose, my Lord?" I asked Anton loud enough to be heard in the front row over the chatter.

"Your Grace," Anton said with aplomb. "I'm sure they wouldn't dare." He stood comfortably with a small smile. "These ladies don't know Court protocol, or how to present themselves and their Houses. I'm almost sure they don't mean to give offense."

The crowd quieted in a slow wave as the ones in front shushed those around them. I waited until the silence went on for a few minutes, then sat up and nodded to Anton.

Anton took a step forward and, with Lady Sara's magical help projecting, said to the assembly, "Thank you for coming Ladies, and notable personages, to his Grace's Court."

Anton made sure to make eye contact as he turned his head, "As his Grace has not posted the formal etiquette of expected behavior, all are forgiven small lapses. Outright rudeness to, his Grace, or others is prohibited in this court." He paused for a moment, to let that sink in, as I'd asked him to. "Please arrange yourselves to pay your respects and introduce yourself to, his Grace, Duke Daniel Montenegro." Anton stepped back to show the gathering they could line up now.

"In the interests of time, I will explain some things while you organize," Anton waited a beat then began his monologue. "His Grace has decided that postings to this court will have offices here. If you need more space, then it is the responsibility of the courtier in question, to hire such facilities in the city, on their own. Court will be held once a month, or sooner if the need is great. If, his Grace, cannot attend in person, then his Chancellor or his Seneschal will take his place."

The line formed quickly as Anton continued to drone on about how requests should be made and what the duties of the functionaries would be.

The presentation and introduction of some four hundred people took hours. Everyone I met blurred together. They were paraded by Lady Sara, then me, and then Anton as quickly as possible. I stopped paying attention after the twentieth person tried to give me an elevator pitch. I stifled a yawn when the last woman crossed the dais.

Anton took a step forward and announced, "The coronation and induction ceremony will be performed here at second bell, followed by the Giving of Oaths, and the celebration banquet. All Heads of Houses are required to attend, or the forfeiture of their holdings will commence. Those choosing to not take Oath with their liege, will also forfeit their lands and station. Court is adjourned."

The nobles and hangers-on filed their way out of the throne room, the way they came in. I left through the door blocked from view by my throne.

Anton, Sara, and I nearly fell into the chairs in the sitting room that we'd normally wait in for court functions.

Servants offered each of us food and drinks as a late night repast. I took a sip of my whisky and said, "That went well."

Anton smiled, but Sara asked, "How so, your Grace?"

"No one died," Anton said as he lifted his glass of red wine.

Sara nearly spit her wine across the table. "What?!" She coughed out.

Anton then began to regale her of my time in Plav. Anton and Sara and I talked for another hour. I started to nod off, so I set my empty glass down, and announced, "I'm off to bed. Big day tomorrow."

"Sure you won't get lost again, your Grace?" Sara asked. She didn't like me gallivanting about either.

"Meh," I held my hand out, palm down turned my wrist in a so-so gesture. "Sixty percent sure."

She scowled at me.

"I didn't run away before, and I'm not going to do it now."

She crossed her arms.

"No, I'm not going to apologize. There is no way either of you would have let me go alone if you had a say in the decision."

Sara looked over at Anton, he just shrugged.

"Good night, my Lady," I turned to Anton and caught a napkin to the face.

Chapter 24

The morning dawned bright and cool. The seasons turned inexorably and autumn fast approached. The port was crammed with ships of types I had no clue of or about. They had masts and sails, that was all I knew about them.

I wore the new robes Mr. Silva made for my coronation today. Red, with black trim and silver embroidery outlining my Phoenix coat-of-arms heraldry on the left breast and back. I'd wanted to wear my black boots, but Anton threatened to quit then and there if I did. So, my slippers susurrated across the stone floors of the Palace. Anton smiled serenely beside me.

I didn't eat much for breakfast that morning, or even lunch later, my stomach bounced and twisted too much for food. I did not have any alcohol. I wanted a clear head for today's events.

My coronation today is for the aristocracy. A week later, I would stand for the acclaim of the people. Both events were important, but if I didn't have the support of the nobles, I faced a long and bloody road to power. The nobility would view it as a usurpation of their authority and wouldn't give up power quietly.

All the boring parties in Plav, hopefully cemented the loyalty of some nobles to my cause. If only a few dissented, then they would work behind the scenes instead of open rebellion. Since the monarchy installed many of them, the Royals would side with the established order, in any long drawn out conflict.

The Cardinal of Mithira assured Anton that the Oath of Fealty, given by a duly appointed representative, would suffice to bind the whole House to mine. Some of them were too old to travel, and I'm sure some couldn't be bothered. Forty of the one hundred Heads of House would be there.

I waited in the sitting room behind the throne for Anton to fetch me. The biggest day of my life, boiled down to a simple ceremony. Nope, not nervous at all.

I took deep breaths and centered myself. Anton opened the door.

"It is time, your Grace."

I nodded my thanks, then made my way up the stairs on the back side of the dais. I couldn't pick out individual words, in the low murmur of voices, that hung like a fog in the throne room. I took one last deep breath, filled with the musty exhalations of humanity, to calm myself. It reminded me of the crushing press, of tourist-filled pyramid tunnels in Egypt, before they banned the practice.

The gathered aristocrats quieted as I made my way to stand before them, in front of the throne. Lady Sara stood to my left. The Cardinal of Mithira stood with Anton to my right. The newly made, Lord Bouvier, held the cup of anointing oil steady in both hands.

The Cardinal put his palms together and said, "Let us pray. Great Goddess Mithira, we beseech you to look down upon us, and witness the man you marked to…" The Cardinal droned on for a long time. He didn't change his inflection, or cadence, like an experienced public speaker might. His monotonous monotone nearly put me, and many in the crowd, to sleep.

"…And do you, Daniel Hawthorne del Montenegro," The holy man, addressing me personally, brought my attention back to the here and now. "Take Oath, under the ever watchful gaze of our Holy Mother, to provide succor in your lands to the followers of our Goddess?"

I nodded and said, "I do so swear."

"To treat all under the law equally?"

"I do so swear."

"Will you elevate, and enrich those sworn to you, and through you, to majestic Mithira?"

"I do so swear."

A soft golden divine aura surrounded us, connecting the Cardinal and I. The gathered nobles gasped as they witnessed the Binding of my Oath, to the Goddess. Many worshiped Mithira, but never witnessed Acts and Miracles, and most of the attendees were suitably impressed by the display.

After the glow faded from us, the Cardinal turned and accepted the cup from Anton. Lady Sara draped the royal purple Stole of Office across my shoulders. The broad band of cloth hung down evenly, just below my knees, with gold embroidered symbols that clashed horribly with my robes.

Lord Anton ceremonially handed over with both hands the Scepter of Office. It looked more like a cane, than a scepter, made of ebony with an orb of polished black stone with gold mountings that fit comfortably in my palm.

The Cardinal murmured a benediction over the oil. He then placed his palm on the top of my head and mumbled something again. After that, he dipped two fingers into the oil, then painted a symbol on my forehead. Another dip, and he pressed the oil onto my lips.

The holy man passed the cup back to Anton, dipped his fingers again, then grabbed my marked hand, with his oil free left hand. He traced the oil along the pattern etched into my skin, painting the black discoloration with anointing oil. The Cardinal took a step back when he finished, pressed his palms together, and raised his gaze to the ceiling murmuring the whole while.

Divine light speared from above and enveloped me. The light

physically pressed down on me, and made my skin tingled uncomfortably. The oil absorbed into the flesh of my lips and brow. On my hand, the oil burned its way into me. The black marking slowly turned the red of blood. Intricacies previously hidden, rose to prominence within the bands. Loops and whorls shifted and crawled as the main design of three interlocked rings separated, into a Malfatti circle, with the point at the base of my knuckles. The pain was excruciating. I didn't scream or cry out, but I may have whimpered.

Purple light etched markings along the Scepter. They started from the hand that I, blessedly, could no longer feel. Runes I didn't know the meaning of, formed up to the orb, and a bright indigo Phoenix flashed into existence; perched there as if it was the most natural thing in the world. It looked around curiously then entered the orb. The previously opaque rock, now showing the three-dimensional image of the fiery bird, that looked back at the observer with its head cocked.

And like that, the divine spear of light disappeared leaving no trace. Except for the change to the markings on my hand. I could feel that they extended up my forearm. If I had a dragon tattoo now, I'd shit myself.

As surreptitiously as I could, I lifted my sleeve and took a peek. I did not have a dragon tattoo. I had a freaking awesome Phoenix! The mark glittered in reds and yellows giving it shape and depth. The bird almost seemed to breathe on my arm.

The Cardinal turned to the assembly and, loud enough to echo in the chamber, said, "I present to you, your Lord and liege." He swept his arm around in a grand gesture and pointed at me with his hand, palm up. "Duke Daniel Hawthorne del Montenegro, blessed of Mithira!"

He threw his arms up in a 'V' and shouted, "The time of Oath Taking is upon us! Step forward, and be recognized as a loyal vassal of his Grace, or forfeit your title to live and toil as a commoner forevermore." He lowered his arms and beckoned Lady Lancaster forward, who'd already begun making her way to the dais.

Nobles rushed into place to form a line. A few did not. They sauntered their way over, telling me without words of their importance. Several women, there were no girls here, swayed and sashayed their way by, preening under my gaze. I found it odd that they were willing to marry their children off so young, but wouldn't allow them to swear an oath that would bind their House.

The Cardinal, blessed man that he was, brooked no conversation during the ceremony. Quips and questions went ignored. A press for an answer was met with a glare. When an older woman of House Crane tried to address me personally, the Cardinal turned and said, "My lady, the Oath is quite simple. If this is too much, you may have a proxy stand in for you."

Lady Crane went pale then flushed. Her hands balled at her sides, but she shook her head no, reciting the Oath, "I affirm, Duke Montenegro, as my liege, and swear to obey him as a vassal according to the precepts of Mithira."

We got down to the last twenty ladies waiting when the ceremony came to a grinding halt.

"No!" A tall dark haired woman shouted. "I will not follow the dictates of a man," the amount of scorn that dripped from her lips made several people near her step back. "I, and therefore House Varejão, will not participate in this barbaric farce. Not unless the Duke is willing to submit, as a man should, to the proper order of a woman."

She took a step back and pointed at me. I could feel the gaze of everyone there piercing into my soul.

"Will you be a man and submit?" Lady Varejão asked.

"No."

She didn't look like she expected my answer.

"Then, take a wife from my House," she waved in the general

direction of several women grouped up. "You have already outright rejected several proposals on spurious grounds. You are already showing that you don't have what it takes to rule."

It took me a moment, then I recognized Lady Minerva in that group. She wore a blonde wig now.

This was planned.

"No. I will not wed a child. The idea is disgusting, and the practice is barbaric and unnecessary. Your entire bloodline is fouled by your insistence in this revolting belief," my face had screwed up involuntarily in a disgusted sneer. "Don't take the Oath. I know of one who is more worthy to take over those lands. One who will remain steadfast in their honor for generations to come. "

Lady Varejão's face reddened in fury. She lifted her finger and shouted, "Die!"

A blazing Lance of fire shot out and impacted my shield. The fire washed over me and would have impacted Sara, but she got her own shield of Air up in time to only receive a few scorch marks on her dress.

Anton fled, like I'd previously told him to. Many of the nobles moved back, though they didn't flee. They didn't step in to help either. I grinned.

"Now!" Lady Varejão shouted.

The ambient mana in the room dropped precipitously. The other five women with Varejão, drew as deeply as they could to power their shields. A normal wizard wouldn't be able to channel enough mana to cast a spell. Which was why Varejão drew a dagger and stabbed me. Or my shield, since I still had it up.

"How long can you keep it up?" Varejão asked me with a sneer.

I scoffed, "Longer than you."

She mistimed her strike and fell against the shield and split her lip.

She recovered quickly and wiped the blood away with the back of her hand. "The mana is already running out," she stabbed again. "You will die whimpering in a pool of your own blood." She set the tip of her dagger against the shield and kept up the pressure.

"I guess if I had to, I would rather it be my own blood," I scratched my beard. "A pool of someone else's blood would be gross to lie in."

"You're pathetic. Just die already!" She put her shoulder into it as she pushed at the dagger. My shield held strong.

I looked down at Lady Varejão and shook my head. I looked out at the noble women gathered, watching the scene, some wringing their hands, a few older ones nodded thoughtfully, I said, "I don't care if you like me. I'm not your friend. I am not your confidant." With all eyes on me, no one noticed when Minerva dropped to the floor.

"I don't care if you disagree with me. I don't care if you are vocal about it. We can not truly improve our stations, without discourse. You might have a great idea," another woman dropped to the ground. "But, we might never know, if you fear to express yourself. Hell, I might have a good idea, but the implementation is all wrong." A third woman dropped and the mana in the room increased considerably. Varejão reacted first.

"What have you done?" She screamed as she saw the bodies on the floor.

"What I will not tolerate," I said, ignoring the nearly hysterical woman trying to kill me. "Is an attack on my person, family, or staff." Another woman fell. Her pretty yellow dress fanned out around her.

I pointed up to the portrait of Osvaldo, above the throne, "He made a mistake that saw his family murdered. I buried both of his daughters."

The crowd turned, almost as one, to look at the painting, and the last woman holding the shield fell as she tried to run. Lady Varejão threw her dagger against my shield and ran. She made it several meters before bands of air lifted her up. Legs pressed together, with her arms bound to her side, she floated back with the hem of her skirt fluttering. Her mouth opened, though no sound escaped. I nodded my thanks to Lady Sara. I'd asked her previously, not to interfere, in case something like this happened. The assassination attempt failed, so now she could intervene.

I set the Scepter under my left arm, then bent and picked up the dagger. I pointed out the fifteen House representatives that didn't have the chance to offer their Oath yet.

"Ladies, I am sure there is no one here who can doubt your loyalty," I nodded to them. "But, you know how people are." I smiled to show my commiseration with them. "So, I offer you an opportunity to lay any and all accusations to rest, here and now."

My nobles, including Lady Lancaster, pushed the fifteen women forward. All but two stumbled forward willingly. Those two were magically flung forward to the center of the room, and immolated by dozens of beams, balls, and fans of fire. A brief scream was heard over the sudden roar of flame.

As horrified as I felt, I didn't let it show on my face. To show weakness among these women would mean the death of my legacy, at the least, if they didn't kill me outright.

"Now, my Ladies, each of you will stab Varejão here, once,"

they stared at me appalled. I patted the air awkwardly with the dagger in my hand. "I know, I know." I gave a half shrug, "But, it's the symbolism that's needed here." My gaze hardened to a glare. "You will prove, beyond a shadow of a reasonable doubt, that you were not in league with her. You will draw her blood to show that, not only are you not involved in this plot. But also, that no one would dare ask you to join their schemes, for fear of what you might do to them."

I held up a finger as if I suddenly came up with something, "They wouldn't even dare exclude you, for fear of someone thinking that they themselves were doing it out of nefarious intentions."

I barked a laugh. "Which one of you will go first?"

... to be continued

Printed in Great Britain
by Amazon